Enid Blyton®

SPRINGTIME STORIES

Look out for all of these enchanting story collections by

Enid Blyton

Enid Blyton
SPRINGTIME STORIES

*Hodder
Children's
Books*

HODDER CHILDREN'S BOOKS

This collection first published in Great Britain in 2018 by
Hodder & Stoughton

1 3 5 7 9 10 8 6 4 2

Enid Blyton ® and Enid Blyton's signature are Registered Trademarks
of Hodder & Stoughton Limited
Text © Hodder & Stoughton Limited, 2018
Illustrations © Hodder & Stoughton Limited, 2018
No trademark or copyrighted material may be reproduced without the
express written permission of the trademark and copyright owner.

A CIP catalogue record for this book is available from the British Library.

ISBN 978 1 444 93933 0

Typeset in Caslon Twelve by Avon DataSet Ltd,
Bidford-on-Avon, Warwickshire

Printed and bound in Great Britain by Clays Ltd, St Ives plc

The paper and board used in this book are made from wood
from responsible sources

MIX
Paper from
responsible sources
FSC® C104740

Hodder Children's Books
An imprint of
Hachette Children's Group
Part of Hodder and Stoughton
Carmelite House
50 Victoria Embankment
London EC4Y 0DZ

An Hachette UK Company
www.hachette.co.uk
www.hachettechildrens.co.uk

Contents

The Cross Shepherd

The Cross Shepherd

DICK WHEELED his car out of the shed and got into the driving seat. It was a very nice little car, bright red with silver wheels, and he was very proud of it. It had room for him at the front, and for one more rather small passenger.

The car had a hooter, and two lights in front that you could switch on. Dick worked it with pedals, and could get along very fast indeed. He raced off down the lane at top speed.

'I'm going to see the lambs jumping about in the field!' he called to his mother. 'I'll be back in good time for lunch.'

He was soon at the big field where the lambs played around the mother sheep. Dick loved to watch them, for they were really very funny. They sometimes jumped on to the top of their mothers – then the big sheep got angry and shook them off.

Dick left his car outside the gate and climbed over into the field. The lambs knew him and came running up. Dick picked one up and cuddled it.

Then a cross voice suddenly came over the field and made Dick jump.

'Put that lamb down! And get out of the field!'

Dick put the lamb down quickly. He looked to see who was shouting, and he saw a bent old shepherd standing at the door of his hut on the other side of the field. The shepherd was waving his stick at Dick as if he meant to hit him with it.

'I wasn't hurting the lamb!' called Dick. 'I was only hugging it!'

'You might drop it and break its leg!' shouted back the cross shepherd. 'I haven't sat up all night long in the cold winter with my lambs just to let a tiresome boy frighten them and hurt them! You get out of the field – you'll be leaving the gate open next, and letting all the sheep into the road. Be off with you!'

'I couldn't leave the gate open because I always climb over it!' shouted back Dick.

'Now don't you stand there talking to me like that!' said the old shepherd, and he took two or three steps across the field. Dick was really afraid of him, and he ran to the gate, climbed over it, and was soon in his car. He pedalled off down the lane to the hills, thinking that the old shepherd was a very horrid man.

He drove his little car quite a long way, following the paths that ran over the hills. Then he began to feel hungry, so he knew it was time for his lunch.

He pedalled back. It was mostly downhill, so he was soon able to take his feet off the hurrying pedals and put them on the little ledges inside the car, pretending that he really was driving it, just as his father drove the big car.

He came to a little bridge over a stream and stopped for a moment to get out of the car and lean over the side of the bridge to see if there were any fish in the water.

There were no fish – but there was something else! There was a little lamb, struggling to get out of the stream!

'There's a lamb fallen into the water!' said Dick, in surprise. 'The banks are so steep just here – it must have been a horrid fall. Poor little thing! Whatever can I do to help it?'

Dick ran down to the side of the stream. He looked at the water, which was fairly deep. He could see that the lamb would soon drown if he did not get it out. But the banks of the stream were so steep that it would be very difficult indeed to reach the lamb.

Dick thought for a moment. No – there was absolutely nothing else to do but to jump right into the water, lift up the lamb, and then try to climb out again. He would get very wet but it couldn't be helped.

So into the water he jumped. Splash! It was nearly up to his waist! The lamb was caught against an old branch that had fallen into the water and become fixed against the bridge. Dick waded to it.

He lifted the lamb up gently and put it round his neck as he had seen the shepherd do when he wanted to carry a lamb and yet keep his hands free. Then he turned to climb out of the stream. It was very difficult.

He lifted the lamb off his shoulders first and laid it down on the bank. Then he tried to scramble up the steep slope. At last he managed to climb up, and he bent over the lamb.

It could not walk. Dick saw that something had hurt its two front legs. Perhaps they were broken. The lamb lay there looking up at him out of frightened eyes.

'You are begging me for mercy,' said Dick, 'but you needn't. I only want to help you!'

He put the lamb over his shoulder again, meaning to carry it all the way back to the farm and come back for his car later. But the lamb was well grown and very heavy. Dick knew he couldn't possibly carry it very far. It couldn't walk – so what was he to do?

'I know!' he said suddenly, to the surprised lamb.

'You shall be the passenger in my car! I can drive you back easily then.'

He put the lamb carefully on the seat next to the wheel. Then he climbed into the driving seat and took hold of the wheel. His wet feet found the pedals and off he went. The lamb lay beside him, feeling more and more surprised, but it trusted this boy with the gentle hands, and was no longer quite so afraid.

People were most astonished to see a lamb as a passenger in Dick's little car! They turned and stared in amazement.

'Did you see that?' they said to one another. 'That boy had a lamb in his car!'

'Oh dear!' said Dick to himself, as he pedalled along. 'I've got to go and see that cross old shepherd now. I can't just put the lamb into the field and hope he will see it, because he mightn't notice it was hurt, and it does need its legs mended. But surely he would notice by the evening! Shall I just put the lamb through a hole in the hedge and leave it there without saying anything?'

Dick looked at the lamb. It looked back at him. It had a little black nose and wide-staring eyes. Dick liked it very much, and he suddenly knew quite certainly that he couldn't push the little creature through the hedge and leave it. He must take it to the shepherd, even though he might be shouted at.

He stopped his car outside the gate. He took the lamb in his arms, opened the gate, shut it behind him, and walked over the field towards the shepherd's hut. The sheep set up a great baaing when they saw him, and the old shepherd at once appeared at the door of his hut. When he saw Dick carrying one of the lambs again, he went red with rage.

'Didn't I tell you to leave my lambs alone!' he yelled. 'Didn't I tell you to get out of my field! You wait till I catch you, you tiresome boy!'

But Dick didn't run away. He went on towards the shepherd, his heart beating fast. The shepherd raised his stick as if he was going to beat Dick, but the boy called to him.

'Wait! Wait! This lamb of yours is hurt! I found it

in the stream, and its legs are hurt. It must have slipped out of the field and run away.'

The shepherd at once took the lamb from Dick. He looked at its legs. 'They're broken,' he said.

'Can you mend them?' asked Dick anxiously.

'They'll mend themselves if I see to them now,' said the shepherd. 'You can help me if you like.'

'Oh, thank you,' said Dick. He followed the shepherd into the hut, and together the two of them gently bound up the little hurt legs. The shepherd made clever wooden splints that he bound fast to each leg. The lamb did not make a sound, but lay quite still, looking up at the two who were caring for it.

'You're wet,' said the shepherd to Dick.

'Yes. I had to jump in the stream to get the lamb,' said Dick.

'This lamb is heavy,' said the shepherd. 'Surely you didn't carry it all the way here from the stream?'

'No. I couldn't,' said Dick. 'I brought it along in my little car. It was my passenger! But I was afraid of bringing the lamb to you because you shouted at me this morning and were very cross.'

'Ah! I didn't know then what sort of a boy you were,' said the old shepherd. 'I get boys in here that break down my hedges and frighten my sheep. So I turn them out of my field. But you can come every day, if you like, and you and I will sit here and watch the lambs playing. I can tell you many a strange tale about lambs and sheep.'

'Oh, thank you,' said Dick. 'Now I must go home to my lunch. I'll come again tomorrow.'

'You come and have lunch with me tomorrow,' said the old shepherd. 'I'll get my wife to make us a picnic lunch, and we'll talk together. I could do with a boy like you for company sometimes!'

Dick went home proudly. The cross shepherd wanted him for a friend! No other boy had ever been able to make friends with the old chap – but Dick could go and have lunch with him the next day.

Now the two are fast friends – and the lamb is quite better. It frisks up to meet Dick whenever it sees the boy coming along in his car – and do you know, it lets him take it for a ride once a week down to the village. It sits beside Dick, just like a proper passenger.

You should see how everyone stares!

The Disobedient Bunny

The Disobedient Bunny

ONCE UPON a time there was a little bunny called Koo. He was the dearest, softest, prettiest little bunny on all the hillside, and his mother and father were very proud of him. But he was terribly naughty. Nobody could think why, because all his brothers and sisters were very obedient little bunnies, and always did what they were told.

'Don't go out on the hillside until the sun has gone,' Koo's mother would say to them all. 'It isn't safe until then.'

And they would rub their wet little noses against her soft sides and say, 'No, Mother, we won't.'

All except Koo. He wouldn't promise not to do anything, just in case he should find he wanted to do it after all. And his mother would suddenly look round and say, 'Where's Koo?'

Nobody knew! He had slipped off along the dark little passage and up into the soft, fresh air of the hillside.

His mother would fetch him back and scold him, and tell him a big man would come and shoot him, but he didn't seem to care a bit.

But one day something happened to Koo, and I'll tell you what it was.

That morning, very early, he and his brothers and sisters and mother and father were all sitting on the grass, busily washing themselves. Koo finished first, and he sat up straight on his hind legs and looked at the country which lay all around.

He had never been allowed to go any farther than a short distance round about his hole, but now he felt very curious to know what the world was like a bit farther off.

Away down at the bottom of the hill stood a wood, cool and green in its early summer dress. Koo thought it looked really lovely.

'Mother,' he said, 'may I go down there?'

'Good gracious no, whatever next!' said his mother in surprise.

'Why not, Mother? Why can't I go?' he asked.

'Because it's too far from our hole,' said his mother. 'You'd get lost, and then a man would catch you.'

'What would he do with me?' asked Koo.

'He would cook you and eat you!' answered his mother.

'What does "cook" mean?' asked Koo, who never ate anything but raw grass.

'You'd be put into a big pot with water in, and hung over a fire till you got hotter and hotter and were ready to eat!' said his mother, getting tired of his questions. 'It's terrible to be cooked, so I've heard. Now it's time to go in – and remember, all of you, never go down to the wood until you are big and strong enough to look after yourselves properly.'

Now Koo felt quite certain that he was old enough to look after himself, and he longed to know what was down in that lovely, cool-looking wood.

How nice it would be to lie there, hidden in the grass all day, instead of being down in our stuffy hole! he thought.

And the disobedient bunny waited until no one was looking – then off he went! He scurried down the hillside in the sunshine, his little bobtail gleaming white as snow.

At last he came to the wood. It was very cool, very shady, and very green. The grass tasted most delicious. Little shoots of bracken were growing up here and there, and Koo ate those too, and thought how silly his mother was to say he was not to leave his home.

'When I've had enough to eat, I'll lie down under that bramble bush,' said Koo to himself. 'It smells nice, and it will be lovely to sleep in the open air.'

Soon he had eaten so much that he really couldn't nibble another blade of grass. He wriggled beneath the brambles and found a nice, soft, dry bed for himself.

'I wish the others were here,' said Koo, suddenly feeling a little bit lonely. 'Mother was quite wrong about being caught and cooked. Why, I've not seen anybody at all except bees and butterflies. Caught and cooked indeed!'

Just at that moment there was a stir and a flutter somewhere nearby. And you'd never guess what the poor little bunny heard someone say.

'Cook Koo! Cook Koo! Cook Koo!'

Koo could hardly believe his ears! Cook Koo? Cook him? How dreadful! Somebody must have seen him. Then his mother was right, after all! Koo lay still as still and listened.

There it was again, nearer this time.

'Cook Koo! Cook Koo!'

Koo dashed out from the bramble bush and fled, trembling, through the wood. He came to a low hazel bush and hid himself there. But there was somebody else near there, saying the same thing!

'Cook Koo! Cook Koo!'

Off went Koo again, as frightened as could be. But,

oh dear! The wood seemed to be full of people telling each other to cook Koo. First one called it out, then another, and whichever way Koo turned he heard it.

'I don't want to be cooked!' he wept. 'I'm only a wee bunny. Don't cook me, I want to go home!'

'Cook Koo! Cook Koo! Cook Koo!' said somebody in the trees nearby.

Then Koo suddenly saw the hillside he had scampered down earlier in the day! What a piece of luck! Up he went, faster than he had ever scampered before, longing to reach home before anyone could cook him. And behind him he heard 'Cook Koo' getting fainter and fainter.

His mother was waiting anxiously beside the hole, looking for her naughty little bunny. She was very glad to see him, and could hardly bear to scold him, she was so happy to have him again.

Koo told her all about his dreadful adventure.

'They kept calling out to each other to cook me!' he said. 'Wasn't it horrible of them, Mother? If I hadn't run very fast indeed, they might have cooked me, mightn't they? I'll never be disobedient again, never!'

Koo didn't know what his mother was smiling at, but I expect you do. Wasn't he a silly little bunny to be frightened by the cuckoos! But still, he was never disobedient again, so his adventure did some good after all!

The
Easter Chickens

The Easter Chickens

TOMMY WAS staying with Auntie Susan and Uncle Ben at the farm for Easter. Mummy and Daddy had gone away for a holiday by themselves, and Tommy was sorry because he did so like Easter at home. There were coloured Easter eggs on the breakfast table to eat then – and chocolate ones too – and perhaps a fluffy yellow chick tied to one egg, or a little rabbit.

I don't expect Auntie Susan or Uncle Ben know what a little boy likes at Easter, thought Tommy. *I don't expect they will buy me any eggs at all. I wish I was at home with Mummy and Daddy!*

Sure enough, when Easter morning came and

Tommy ran downstairs to breakfast, there was no coloured egg for him in his egg cup – only just an ordinary brown egg laid by Henny-Penny, the brown hen.

Tommy looked to see if there were any chocolate eggs for him – but there wasn't even a very small one. He felt very sad.

'Sit down and eat your breakfast, Tommy,' said Auntie Susan. 'We must get on because I have a lot of things to do today.' Auntie Susan always had a lot of things to do. So did Uncle Ben. Perhaps that was why they hadn't remembered his Easter eggs, Tommy thought. He remembered how he had seen a little yellow chick in the sweet shop yesterday down in the village. It was carrying an egg. He would have liked that very much. He wondered if he should ask Auntie Susan if she would buy it for him, but he decided that he mustn't ask for things. She said if he was nice enough, people would always buy him things because they loved him without being asked.

I may not have been nice enough, Tommy thought.

So, instead of being sulky and disappointed, he tried to be extra nice to Auntie Susan, and ate his egg without dropping a single bit of the yellow part on the tablecloth.

'Can I go on any errands for you, Auntie Susan?' he asked, when he had finished breakfast.

'I think Uncle Ben wants you to go down to the hencoops with him,' said Auntie. 'I'm coming too.'

So they all three went down to the hencoops. There were four of these, with four brown hens sitting on thirteen eggs each.

And do you know, when they came to the first hencoop, some of the eggs had hatched! Yes – and there were three yellow chicks running about saying, 'Cheep-cheep-cheep!' as loudly as they could.

'Oh!' said Tommy, delighted. 'Look at those dear little chicks, Auntie! Do look at them! They are much sweeter than the toy ones I saw in the shop yesterday! And oh, look – they have got something tied to their backs – whatever are they carrying?'

'Look and see,' said Uncle Ben with a laugh.

So Tommy crouched down and peeped to see what they were carrying. The chicks had gone into the coop with their mother and it was difficult to see one.

At last one of them came out again – and what *do* you suppose it had got on its back? A little chocolate egg! Fancy that!

'It's carrying an egg, just like the little chick at the sweet shop!' cried Tommy. 'Oh, who is the egg for, Auntie Susan?'

'It's for a nice little boy I know, called Tommy,' said Auntie Susan, laughing. 'That chick has an egg from *me*, Tommy – and that one has an egg for you from Uncle Ben – and the third one has an egg from Mummy and Daddy. It came for you yesterday, and we kept it till Easter Day. Then when the chicks hatched out, we thought you would like to have eggs and chicks together – really proper Easter chicks this time!'

'Auntie! Are the yellow chicks for me as well? Oh, I am *so* pleased!'

Uncle Ben caught the chicks and took off the

chocolate eggs for Tommy. The little boy cuddled the soft cheeping chicks. Their little bodies were so warm. He loved the tiny creatures – and they were his very own!

'Will they grow into hens and lay me eggs?' he asked.

'Oh yes!' said Auntie Susan. 'You shall take them home with you next week when you go – real, live Easter chicks, Tommy, for your very own!'

'This is the nicest Easter I've ever had,' said Tommy. 'And I thought it wasn't going to be. What *will* Mummy say when I take home my Easter chicks!'

Tommy still has his chicks – but they are growing into brown hens now and will soon lay him eggs – one for his own breakfast each morning, one for his mummy, and one for his daddy. Don't you think he is lucky?

Mr Quink's Garden

Mr Quink's Garden

ONE FINE day, not long ago, Mr Brown took his wife and children, Jenny and Tom, for a day out in the country.

'It will be a lovely day,' said Mr Brown. 'The countryside is beautiful at this time of year. We'll have lots of fun together. Let's hurry up and pack a big picnic.'

So they made ham and tomato sandwiches, and packed them into lunch boxes. They took two bottles of homemade lemonade, and packed oranges and bananas into a basket with the bottles. They took a large fruitcake and a packet of biscuits. And last of all they took four bars of chocolate and a bag of sweets.

It was a lovely day when they set off in the car. The sun shone and the sky was as blue as the bluebells in the woods. Birds sang in the hedges, and the banks were yellow with primroses.

The Brown family were happy, sitting and looking at the scenery.

They got out of the car at last and walked into the woods. The sun was so hot that they were glad of the shade. Tom and Jenny ran on in front, shouting to their mother to look at the bluebells. Mr and Mrs Brown carried the bags and basket.

'Look for a nice place to sit, Jenny,' called Mrs Brown.

Presently they found just the spot. It was the prettiest place in the wood – and, although they did not know it, it was the garden belonging to Mr Quink, the brownie. He lived in the old oak tree under whose branches the Brown family sat. He had a close-fitting door in the trunk of the tree and a small window with a tiny curtain of moss. No one knew he lived there – except the little folk of course – for Mr Quink never showed himself to ordinary people.

Now Mr Quink was very proud of his garden and he worked there every night. There was a tiny stream running through it, and he had planted flowers neatly along each bank. He had arranged cushions of moss so that his friends could sit on them when they came to visit him. He had three patches of bluebells, the finest in the wood – and a white bluebell, which is a very lucky flower. Mr Quink planted honeysuckle in one corner, and a nook of violets close by, so that whoever sat there could smell the sweet scent of the hidden violets. Everything in the garden was neat, tidy and beautiful.

No wonder the Browns thought it was lovely! They sat down under the tree and put their basket by the trunk. They didn't know they were in a brownie's garden, as there was no fence or hedge round it.

'Let's have our lunch now,' said Mrs Brown, beginning to unpack the things. Soon they were all munching happily. They drank the lemonade. It was delicious.

'Let's put the bottles over there and throw stones at them,' said Mr Brown.

'But won't the broken pieces be dangerous?' said Mrs Brown.

'Who for? No one ever comes here,' said Mr Brown.

So they set up the bottles and threw stones at them, and soon the bottles were smashed to bits, and pieces of glass lay all over the ground. Mr Brown unfolded his newspaper. 'I'm going to have a rest,' he said. 'Run along and play, children.'

Little by little the lovely garden belonging to Mr Quink began to look dreadful. The brownie peeped out of his tiny window in the oak tree and saw with dismay what was happening.

He saw Mrs Brown peel oranges for the children and throw the peel on the ground. He saw the children eating bananas and throwing the skins at one another. And he saw Mr Brown throw empty sweet wrappers under the honeysuckle bush.

The Brown family stayed there all afternoon. It was so peaceful, and the birds sang sweetly. They had tea and then it was time to go home.

Mrs Brown looked round at the mess, and couldn't help feeling a bit sorry about it.

'Are there any litter bins?' she asked. 'Perhaps we ought to clear this mess up.'

'There aren't any, Mum,' said Tom. 'This is quite a wild part of the wood. I don't suppose anyone comes here but us. Still, our teacher always tells us not to spoil the country – don't you think we should take our rubbish back home with us?'

'I'm not carrying all that litter back,' said Mr Brown. He was rather a selfish man. 'Leave it here. No one will ever know.'

'Mummy, let's take these bluebells home with us,' cried Jenny. 'And let's dig up the primroses and violets, and some of the moss. We can plant them in our garden at home!'

So they dug up Mr Quink's finest primroses, violets and moss, and picked all his bluebells – and then they found the lucky white bluebell! So they dug it up and put it in the basket too. Then home they went.

Mr Quink opened his front door and crept out. When he saw his beautiful garden scattered with broken glass, orange peel, banana skins, cardboard boxes, empty bags and packets, sweet papers and sheets of newspaper – when he saw his lovely plants gone and his moss spoilt, he sat down on a stone and cried big tears. But when he found his white bluebell gone he was very angry! He called a meeting of all the brownies in the wood and they came to see his spoilt garden. Most of them had complaints and grumbles too.

'Some people left all their horrible paper bags in my field the other day,' said Nod, an old brownie.

'And some boys threw broken bottles into my stream, and I cut my feet when I paddled there,' said Doolin, a small, bright-eyed brownie.

'But these Browns are the worst of the lot,' said Mr Quink fiercely. 'Look at this mess! Whatever shall I do with it?'

'Well, the Browns have a neat little garden,' said Hoodle, a sharp-eyed brownie who travelled a good deal. 'As all this mess belongs to them, why not take it back to them and put it into their own garden?'

'That's a good idea!' said all the brownies at once. 'They don't seem to mind litter and rubbish and mess – so maybe they won't bother about broken bottles and papers and peel in their own garden.'

'I can give them some newspapers I've picked up in my field,' said Nod.

'And I can give them a sackful of broken glass,' said Doolin.

'We'll go tonight and dump everything in the Browns' garden,' said everyone. 'How pleased they will be to get such a nice lot of rubbish back!'

That night they took their sacks and made their way from the wood, riding on the back of the midnight owl who flies to and from the town.

When they got to the Browns' garden they landed on the grass and opened their sacks. They shook glass all over the neat lawn. They threw newspapers where the wind could blow them around. They scattered paper and boxes and peel and skin here and there. Just as they were going, Mr Quink stopped and pointed to something.

'Look!' he said. 'My lucky white bluebell! I'll take that back with me.'

'And see – here's a lupin plant just flowering!' said Nod. 'I haven't got one of those at home. As the Browns took your flowers, Quink, they probably wouldn't mind us taking theirs. I'd like that lupin!'

In a few minutes the brownies were digging up all the nicest things in the Browns' garden, and then off they went again on the owl, their sacks empty of rubbish but full of lovely plants. They were delighted.

In the morning, when Mr Brown woke up and looked out of the window, he got such a shock! His garden was a wreck! The plants were gone, the lawn was scattered with broken glass, and all kinds of rubbish blew about or lay on the flowerbeds.

'Just look at that!' said Mr Brown fiercely. 'Now who's done that, I should like to know?'

Mrs Brown jumped out of bed and gazed at the dreadful garden. Tears came into her eyes, for she loved her little garden. 'Oh, how could anyone be so horrid?' she said.

Tom and Jenny were angry too. 'What a terrible mess,' said Jenny. 'Why don't people clear up their litter properly instead of throwing it into our garden?'

Mr Brown told the policeman, who wrote a lot of things down in his notebook and said he would keep a watch on the garden and see it didn't happen again. And Tom and Jenny spent the whole morning clearing up the mess and making the garden neat. Mr Brown had to buy more plants in place of the ones that had gone, and he was very angry about it.

The next night, although the policeman watched carefully, someone he didn't see came and emptied all sorts of rubbish in the Browns' garden again! It was most extraordinary because although the policeman saw the rubbish being thrown about the garden he couldn't see who was throwing it!

The brownies were invisible to him, for he didn't

believe in fairies. He was frightened and ran all the way back to the police station.

And do you know, the brownies still come every other night or so and give to the Browns all the rubbish that people leave in the countryside. Their garden is a dreadful sight and they can't do anything about it.

In fact, Jenny is beginning to wonder if it can be the little folk who are doing it – and she wishes her family hadn't been so untidy in the wood that day!

'I shall put up a notice to say we're sorry and won't spoil the country again,' said Jenny. 'Then the little folk will stop bringing us rubbish.' So she is going to do that tonight – and then the brownies will have to choose someone else's garden. I hope it won't be yours!

But I'm sure you are not like the Browns, are you? You know how to behave when you go to the country, so *your* garden will be safe!

Slowcoach Sammy

Slowcoach Sammy

SLOWCOACH SAMMY belonged to a family of brownies, and you can guess why he had such a funny name. He was such a slowcoach! He was last in everything, and his mother, Mrs Trot-About, got quite cross with him.

'You're always last, Sammy,' she said. 'I call the others, and they come running at once. But you stay behind and make me feel so cross.'

Poor old Slowcoach Sammy! He missed the bus when he went shopping. He missed the train when Mrs Trot-About took the family to see Aunt Twinkle. He even missed the elephant when he went to the zoo, so he couldn't have his ride.

One day his mother called to all her family, 'Come with me. I want you to do some gardening. I have lettuce and mustard and cress seeds, and we will plant them all in our garden so that we shall have plenty to eat in the summer.'

Tickle came running. Humps rushed up. Jinky came round the corner at top speed. Ricky arrived panting. But Slowcoach Sammy wasn't to be seen, as usual.

'He's watching a spider making its web at the front gate,' said Tickle.

'Sammy, Sammy, Sammy! Hurry up or you won't have time to do any gardening!' cried Mrs Trot-About. 'I've only twenty minutes to spare to help you all plant your seeds.'

But Slowcoach Sammy didn't hurry. He watched the spider till she had finished her web. Then he watched a worm wriggling out of a hole. Then he watched a bird flying right up into the sky. At last he got to his mother and his brothers and sisters.

But they had finished their gardening and were picking up their spades to put them back into the shed.

'What a slowcoach you are, Sammy!' said Mrs Trot-About. 'I called you ages ago! Now we have finished, and all the seeds are planted.'

'I want to plant some seeds too,' said Sammy.

'Well, you can't. The others have planted them all – there they are, neatly labelled in rows,' said his mother, waving her spade to the garden beds.

'I do want to plant some seeds!' wept Sammy. 'I want some plants of my own too. I do want to plant some seeds!'

'It's no use making that noise,' said his mother. 'You should have come when you were called. There are no more seeds at all.'

Sammy went off to cry in the playroom. He hunted in the cupboard to see if there were any packets of seeds left. And at last he came to a little packet that rattled when he shook it. He opened it. Inside lay a great many tiny coloured round things.

'Seeds!' said Slowcoach Sammy, delighted. 'Seeds

that everybody else has forgotten. I'll go and plant them straight away, and won't the others look blue when they see I have got seeds coming up after all!'

Well, if Sammy had looked closely at that packet, he would have seen that they were tiny beads belonging to his sister Jinky! But he didn't. He just hurried out to plant them.

He made little holes along his garden bed and shook the beads inside. He covered them up well. He watered them, and patted down the ground nicely. He was very pleased with himself.

'They can call me slowcoach all they like, but they'll be surprised when they see how much nicer my seeds are than theirs!' said Sammy to himself. 'My word, with seeds coloured as brightly as that I ought to have flowers all colours of the rainbow!'

Well, the other seeds began to come up, showing a green mist in the beds – but Slowcoach Sammy's didn't peep through at all! He went out to look twenty times a day, but it wasn't any use – he didn't see a single green head coming through the soft brown earth.

He was so disappointed. The seeds of the others grew and grew – but Sammy's didn't come up at all. (I'm not really surprised. Are you?)

Mrs Trot-About was sorry to see Sammy so unhappy about his seeds. He had told her that he had found a forgotten packet in the cupboard, and she thought they were mustard and cress or lettuce. She couldn't think why they didn't come up.

'I shall dig them up and see what's the matter with them,' said Slowcoach Sammy to the others.

'Maybe they are slowcoaches like you!' said Jinky. They all came with him and watched him dig up his bed. He turned up heaps of the little round coloured things and picked them out of the earth.

'Just look!' he said. 'They haven't put out any root or shoot or bud or leaf! What bad seeds they are!'

Then the others began to laugh. How they laughed! 'What the matter?' asked Sammy, in surprise. 'Do you think my seeds are so funny?'

'Yes, we do!' laughed Ricky. 'What did you expect to grow from those seeds, Sammy? Necklace flowers and bracelet buds? They are tiny little beads!'

Poor Slowcoach Sammy! He stood and stared at his bead-seeds and tears trickled down his red cheeks. No wonder they wouldn't grow! He had planted beads!

'Never mind, Sammy, you can share my lettuces,' said kind Jinky.

'It's not the same to share,' said Sammy. 'I want seeds of my own.'

'Then you mustn't be such a little slowcoach next time,' said his mother. 'We'll try and help you not to be.'

And what do you think his family say to him when they see Sammy being slow? They say, 'Hi, Sammy! Your beads will never grow unless you hurry up!'

Then, my goodness, how he hurries and scurries!

They Can't Catch
Brer Rabbit!

They Can't Catch
Brer Rabbit!

'YOU KNOW,' said Brer Fox to Brer Wolf, 'it's just about time we caught Brer Rabbit, Brer Wolf. He's getting so uppity these days, he'll soon be ordering us about!'

'Well, let's catch him, then,' said Brer Wolf. 'We'll think of a plan. Shall we set a trap for him?'

'I've got a better idea than that,' said Brer Fox. 'We'll catch him in a net!'

'How can we do that?' said Brer Wolf. 'He'll see a net.'

'Now, you listen,' said Brer Fox. 'We'll have a hunting party, see? You can bring a net to catch butterflies, and I'll bring one to catch fish. And we'll tell Brer Rabbit to bring a net, too, and catch what he likes. We'll say that we'll bring the lunch – he needn't bother to bring any.'

'And when he's not looking we'll clap our nets down over him – and that will be the end of old Brer Rabbit!' said Brer Wolf, pleased. 'A mighty fine idea, Brer Fox!'

Well, the two of them told Brer Rabbit about their hunting party, and Brer Rabbit listened with both his ears.

'You bring your net and catch what you like,' said Brer Fox. 'We'll bring ours, too. And don't you bother about any food, Brer Rabbit. We'll bring that, and we'll share it with you.'

'Well, that's mighty kind of you,' said Brer Rabbit. 'I'll be pleased to come. And don't forget I like carrot sandwiches, will you?'

Now, when the day for the hunting party came, Brer Rabbit made up his mind he'd be along at the meeting place quite early. It seemed a bit funny that

Brer Fox and Brer Wolf should be so friendly with him all of a sudden. So off he went early, and crawled under a bush to wait, taking his net with him.

Presently along came Brer Fox and Brer Wolf, each with most enormous nets. 'Heyo, Brer Fox!' said Brer Wolf. 'My, you ought to be able to catch old Brer Rabbit in that! That net of yours is big enough to catch an elephant.'

'And yours is strong enough to catch a tiger!' said Brer Fox. 'Now, we must each pretend to be looking for fish or for butterflies as soon as we see old Brer Rabbit coming. You wait about by those flowers, and I'll sit down at the stream here. He's late.'

Oho! thought Brer Rabbit to himself. *I'm late, am I? It's a good thing I was early, it seems to me!*

'Did you bring a picnic lunch?' called Brer Wolf to Brer Fox.

'Yes. I'll put it down here,' shouted back Brer Fox, and he put down a nice, fat basket of food, not far from Brer Rabbit's bush. The smell of it reached Brer Rabbit's nose, and it was very good.

Brer Wolf danced about among the flowers with his net, and Brer Fox swished about in the stream with his. They both kept an eye open for Brer Rabbit, but he didn't come, and he didn't come. He was looking through a hole in his bush at that picnic basket and wishing he could feast on what was inside it.

He waited till Brer Fox and Brer Wolf were looking the other way – and then he quietly pushed his net out from under the bush, and put it over the basket. He began to draw it back towards the bush.

He soon got it under the bush, and opened the basket. My, how good everything smelt!

I'll take it home to my family! thought Brer Rabbit. *That's what I'll do!*

So, as bold as brass, he crept out from under the bush, and shouted at Brer Fox and Brer Wolf.

'Heyo, folks! Having a nice party? I hope you'll catch what you went to catch!'

Brer Fox almost fell into the stream when he heard Brer Rabbit shout. Brer Wolf stepped into some nettles and then out again in a hurry.

'Where did you come from?' shouted Brer Fox. 'We've been watching out for you for a long time. We wanted you to go hunting with us. You come here and see what I've caught.'

'I've been hunting under that bush,' said Brer Rabbit. 'You wouldn't believe what I caught!'

He swung his net around and Brer Fox suddenly saw that Brer Rabbit had got his picnic basket in it. He gave an angry yell and rushed at him. Brer Rabbit danced away.

'You're a thief, Brer Rabbit!' cried Brer Fox. 'Yes, that's what you are! You just came to steal our lunch. You didn't come here to catch anything.'

'I did, I did!' shouted Brer Rabbit, dancing round and round a bush and making Brer Fox come after him with his net.

'Well, you tell me what you came to catch, then!' yelled Brer Fox. 'You just tell me.'

Brer Rabbit ran to the hedge and waved his net at Brer Fox. 'You go and catch fish, Brer Fox, and leave me to catch what I want to catch.'

'What are you going to catch? You tell me that!' shouted Brer Fox.

Brer Rabbit leapt right over the hedge. A bus was rumbling up the lane. Brer Rabbit put out his hand and stopped it.

'Heyo, Brer Fox!' he called, as he hopped up on to the step. 'I'm catching the bus. That's what I'm catching. *The bus!*'

And off he went with the picnic basket in his net, laughing so much that he could hardly put his hand into his pocket for the fare!

Biggitty and the Green Hen

Biggitty and the Green Hen

ONCE, BIGGITTY the brownie did a dreadful thing. He crept through a hole in Dame Clucker's fence, slipped inside her henhouse, and stole an egg! Nobody saw him. Nobody knew.

But when Biggitty got back home and looked at the egg, he got a shock! It was bright green! Now the brownie knew it must be an enchanted egg of some sort, and he wondered what to do.

'I'll boil it!' he said. 'If it's boiled it can't do any harm. If it tastes nice I'll have it for my tea.'

So he popped it into a saucepan of boiling water – but after a minute the egg began to sing loudly, *wheeee-ee, wheeee-ee!* And, before Biggitty's astonished eyes it burst with a loud pop – and out sprang a tiny, green hen, complete to the last feather in her tail!

'Oooh!' said Biggitty, and made a grab at it. But the hen dodged neatly to one side. She flew up to the beam in the ceiling and preened her feathers, keeping a sharp eye on Biggitty.

Now Biggitty was not only a dishonest little brownie, but he was also untruthful and not very clean. So the little green hen was not very lucky in her owner. She stayed up in the rafters, watching everything. She saw that Biggitty's hands were dirty. She saw that his nails were simply black. She noticed that his hair had not been brushed. There wasn't a thing she didn't see!

Biggitty didn't at all like the way the little green hen watched him. He glared at her, and said, 'Stare all you like! That won't do me any harm. Wait till I get hold of you!'

'Clucka-lucka-luck!' said the hen, and scratched the back of her head thoughtfully.

A knock came at the door and a pixie put his head in. 'Coming out for a walk, Biggitty?' he called. Before Biggitty could answer, a voice came from the rafters.

'Biggitty hasn't washed behind his ears this morning.'

The pixie stared at Biggitty, laughed and went away. Biggitty was furious. He caught up a broom and tried to sweep the green hen off the beam. But she dodged away and he swept down a great string of onions, that fell round his neck.

'Wait till I get you!' said Biggitty to the clucking hen.

The baker came to the door and looked in. 'Any bread today?'

'Cluck-a-cluck! Biggitty's nails could grow potatoes!' shouted the little green hen. The baker took a look at Biggitty's nails, gave a shudder, and went away. Biggitty could hardly say a word, he was so angry. He shut the door and the windows, and fetched his stepladder. He meant to get that little green hen down! But she flew up the chimney, found a nook there out of the smoke, and stayed there, clucking loudly. And nothing Biggitty could do would get her down. She didn't seem to mind heat or smoke at all.

Dame Twiddle came to call. She sat down on a chair and asked Biggitty if he was well.

'Clucka-lucka-luck!' screamed the hen up the chimney. 'His teeth aren't well because he never cleans them.'

'Dear me!' said Dame Twiddle. 'Is this a new pet of yours, Biggitty?'

'No,' said Biggitty angrily. 'Please go, Dame Twiddle. I'm busy today.'

'Yes! He has got to brush his hair and wash his hands!' said the voice in the chimney. 'Clucka-lucka-luck!'

Dame Twiddle took a quick look at Biggitty's untidy hair and dirty hands and chuckled.

'Well, you've got some good advice!' she said. 'I should take it, Biggitty!'

As soon as she was gone, Biggitty poured some water on the fire. It sizzled loudly and clouds of smoke poured out into the room. Then Biggitty stamped on the embers and what do you suppose he did? He began to climb up the chimney! He *meant* to get that little green hen! Yes, he did!

Up he climbed and up, and came at last to where the little green hen was cosy in her nook. She pecked him, but he took hold of her. He climbed down again, put her into a basket, and took her next door to Dame Clucker.

Dame Clucker opened the door.

'Good afternoon,' said Biggitty. 'I've brought one of your hens back. She must have escaped through the fence.'

'Dear me, that's very, very good of you,' said Dame Clucker, in surprise. She took the basket – but the little green hen flew out and was away in the air before either the brownie or the old dame could catch her.

'Well, well!' said Dame Clucker. 'She's gone! Take an egg from my henhouse, Biggitty, in return for bringing me back the hen.'

'Oh no, thank you!' said Biggitty hurriedly. He

had had quite enough of Dame Clucker's eggs! He ran home in glee. Aha! He had got rid of that wretched bird, and earned a good mark for himself from Dame Clucker!

He set his tea, humming. The postman brought him a letter, and stayed for a chat. Suddenly a voice came from the chimney.

'Clucka-lucka-luck! Biggitty has two big holes in his stockings. I saw his toes poking through when he changed his shoes.'

The postman giggled and went out laughing. Biggitty turned pale with fright and then red with anger. So that horrid, horrid green hen had come back again! He went to the chimney and looked up.

'Are you up there *again*?' he called.

The little green hen scraped about and dislodged a lot of soot that went flying down the chimney and covered Biggitty from head to foot. What a sight he looked!

'Biggitty is very black and dirty! Clucka-luck-luck!' said the hen brightly.

So Biggitty was! He stood storming at the hen. Then he went off to have a bath. He soaped himself well. He washed behind his ears. He cleaned his teeth and his nails. He brushed his wet hair till it lay smooth and shining. He put on clean clothes, for the soot had got into every corner of his other clothes.

Just as he had finished, there came a knock at the door. Tiptoe, the little pixie, looked in.

'Oh!' she said, when she saw Biggitty, 'how smart you look!'

'Clucka-lucka-luck!' screamed the little green hen in the chimney. 'He has washed his hands. He has washed behind his ears. He has cleaned his nails. He has brushed his hair. He has no holes in his stockings.'

Biggitty blushed – but Tiptoe looked at him admiringly. 'What a clean brownie you must be!' she said. 'I will come and have tea with you on Saturday!'

She skipped off. Biggitty *was* pleased to think that such a pretty little pixie should say nice things to him. He went and admired himself in the glass.

'Clucka-lucka-luck!' said the voice in the chimney.

'Biggitty is very conceited! He stares at himself in the glass!'

Biggitty was going to poke a broom up the chimney to try and get down the hen when he stopped himself and thought for a moment.

'No,' he said. 'That bird is only telling the truth. I was pleased just now when it told the truth and said nice things. It is my own fault if it says nasty things! I will see that it only has nice things to say! Aha! That will make it feel blue!'

So Biggitty turned over a new leaf and became a clean and good little brownie. The green hen found nothing but good things to say, and soon she had so little fear of Biggitty that she hopped down the chimney and sat on the arm of his chair beside him.

Now she is his pet! She takes seed from his hand, and lets him stroke her. And when Tiptoe, the pixie, comes to tea the little green hen has a fine time, for they both spoil her thoroughly.

She only says nice things now, and if ever you go to see Biggitty, don't be surprised if you hear a voice from the chimney or the ceiling, will you – saying, 'Biggitty washed his neck well this morning!' Or, 'Biggitty had a bath last night! Clucka-lucka-luck!'

The Runaway Hat

The Runaway Hat

IT ALL happened because the wind blew Jill's hat off. It blew so hard that her straw hat flew off her head, and went bowling over and over down the hill.

'Run after it, Jill!' said Auntie Kate. 'Quick, or it will be lost!'

Jill ran after it, and soon got up to the rolling hat. For a moment it lay still, but just as Jill stooped to pick it up, the wind gave a puff, and sent the hat on again.

What was more annoying still, Jill felt absolutely certain she heard a chuckling laugh, right by her ear.

She looked round. No, nobody was near! Who had

laughed, then? Surely it couldn't have been the wind!

She ran on again after her hat. It was bowling on, far in front of her, jumping over puddles as if it knew it mustn't go into them. Then it lay still again.

'Well!' said Jill. 'I'll get you this time,' and she ran on as fast as she could. She bent down to her hat and caught hold of the brim – but, 'Oh botheration!' said Jill – for the wind jerked the hat out of her hand and sent it flying into the wood at the side of the road. And by her ear came that gurgling chuckle again! Just as if somebody were laughing till the tears ran down his cheeks.

Jill looked all round. No one was near.

'All right,' said Jill. 'I can hear you, Mister Wind! It's jolly mean of you to take away my hat, but I'm going to catch it, so there!' She ran into the wood and looked about for her hat. Yes, there it was, caught in a branch of a tree.

'I'm sure I can climb that!' said Jill, and looked for an easy place to get up.

But would you believe it! No sooner was she

climbing up than the wind blew the hat off the branch and sent it down on the ground again. It really was most tiresome.

Jill climbed down. The hat lay away in the distance, half buried in last year's leaves. Jill decided to stalk it, as a cat stalks a bird.

I believe the hat is helping the wind to tease me! she thought.

So she dodged from tree to tree until she had nearly reached the heap of dead leaves where she thought the hat lay.

Then suddenly out she pounced and caught hold of it.

But it wasn't the hat! It was a great white toadstool that broke in her hands! Jill heard the wind laugh again and saw the hat running away in front of her.

Jill was growing cross. On she went again, determined not to stop running until she caught that hat. She was quickly catching it up. She would soon have it – two or three steps more – a grab – and oh!

The hat had rolled right into a little pond that lay

hidden in a dip in the wood. There it floated, upside down, green with weed and brown with mud.

'Very well,' said Jill. 'You're a very silly hat. I shall leave you there alone. I'm sure I don't want to wear you anymore!'

She thought she heard a laugh behind her. Yes, there it was again, farther off, beyond the nearby trees.

I'll go and catch that rascally wind if I can! thought Jill, and went in the direction of the laugh.

Now and again she heard the chuckling, and each time she ran in the direction it came from. After a while she stood still. She could hear no laughing. The wind was gone.

But hark! What was that contented humming sound? Jill listened. Then she stole towards the hazel trees in front of her, and peeped round them.

What she saw made her stare as if she could not believe her eyes.

She saw a beautiful little glade, full of wild white anemones, each with dainty little frills of green. And they were dancing, every one of them – nodding and swaying, shaking out their little green frills and looking as pretty as a picture.

And kneeling down among them was the wind! He was blowing here and blowing there, making the flowers dance for him in every corner.

Jill watched for a minute. Then she said, 'Mister Wind! Do you know what you have done to my hat?'

The wind turned round in surprise.

'Hello! Why, it's Jill!' He smiled. 'Yes, I blew your hat off for a joke!'

'Well, it's rolled into the pond, and I can't wear it anymore,' said Jill. 'I think it's unkind of you.'

'Oh dear! Oh dear!' said the wind. 'I didn't mean to do that! I must have blown too hard! I'm really very sorry.'

'I don't mind a joke,' said Jill. 'I think jokes are funny, even when they're played on me – but to lose my hat altogether isn't a joke, I can tell you.'

'Well, I'd give you my hat to make up for it,' said the wind, looking very worried, 'only I haven't got one. My brother, the North Wind, blew it away the other day. Would you accept a few of my flowers instead? They're the only ones out, you know, and this is my special garden.'

'They are certainly out very early,' said Jill. 'Yes, I'd like some, please. They'll make up for losing my hat.'

The wind picked her a lovely bunch of the dainty little anemones, told her the way out of the wood, laughed, and vanished.

Jill went back up the hill to her auntie. She showed her the flowers.

'Good gracious, Jill!' she cried. 'Wherever did you find those flowers? I've never seen them out so early in the year before! How perfectly lovely!'

'The wind sent my hat into a pond,' said Jill, 'and gave me these flowers to make up for it. What are they called, Auntie Kate?'

'They're wood anemones,' said Auntie Kate. 'But people always call them windflowers, because they dance so prettily in the wind.'

'So that's why he's got his garden full of them!' said

Jill to herself. 'They're his very own flowers! No wonder they dance so prettily when he blows.'

And I think when you see the windflowers nodding and swaying when the South Wind blows, you will say too that there couldn't be a better name for the little dancing flowers of the spring.

The Surprising
Easter Egg

The Surprising
Easter Egg

ANNA WAS going to a party. She was all ready. She
had on her new pink silk dress, a ribbon round her
hair, her shoes in a bag and a clean handkerchief in
her pocket. She felt so excited, for she loved parties
almost better than anything else.

'Now, it's time you started,' said Mother. 'Goodbye,
Anna. Have a lovely time – and remember to say thank
you very much to Mrs Jones when you leave.'

'I won't forget!' said Anna happily. She ran down
the garden path and out into the lane. What fun it was
to be going to a party! Little Louise Jones's birthday
fell in Easter week this year, and it was going to be a

lovely party, with an Easter egg for everyone to take home. Anna felt very happy.

She skipped down the lane past Mrs White's house. Anna always stopped and looked over the gate at Mrs White's, because she had two lovely Persian cats – blue-grey, with great orange eyes and long thick fur. Anna loved all animals – and wasn't it a pity, she had no pet of her own at all! No dog, no cat, not even a goldfish, lived at Anna's house. No one had thought of letting her have a pet. Anna's mother was not very fond of animals, so she didn't bother about them.

Anna looked over Mrs White's gate, hoping to see one of the lovely Persian cats somewhere in the garden. They loved Anna and always came running to her to be stroked. Anna knew that they had six little kittens just now – and how she longed to see them! But Mrs White was rather a grand sort of lady, and Anna didn't like to ask her if she might go and see the kittens.

There were no cats in the garden at all, so Anna went on her way down the lane, thinking of the party, and wondering if there would be red or yellow jelly, and which she would choose. Halfway down the lane she passed an old tumbledown barn – and as she went by it she heard a noise that made her stop in surprise.

It was the mewing of cats! Now what could they be mewing for in the barn? Anna stopped and looked round. She saw a curious sight! One of Mrs White's Persian cats was coming slowly along under the hedge – and in its mouth it carried one of its kittens! It was holding the kitten by the skin of its neck, as cats do. Anna was so surprised. She watched the cat slip under the hedge, make its way through the wet field, and disappear into the old barn.

The mewing still went on. Anna couldn't understand it. *Mrs White's cat must have taken all her kittens into the barn*, she thought. *What a dreadful place to take them – so damp and cold and dirty! Poor little things!*

Anna found a hole in the hedge and squeezed through it. She went to the barn and peeped in. It was dark and at first she could hardly see anything. Then she discovered where the kittens were.

The mother cat had climbed up a plank, and had put all her six kittens, one by one, on a shelf in the barn. There was a hole in the barn wall just there, and the wind came in. The kittens were cold and frightened. One crawled about the shelf – and then, to Anna's horror, it fell over the edge, bounced on the plank, and rolled to the ground!

It didn't seem to be hurt, but Anna was worried. Suppose they all fell off? Silly mother cat, to put her kittens there!

Oh dear, I shall be late for the party, thought Anna, *and I've got my best dress on. Whatever am I to do? I simply can't leave those kittens there.*

She looked round for a ladder. There was an old one at the end of the barn. Anna dragged it across and put it up against the wall. She went up it and reached the shelf where the kittens were. There were five there – and one on the floor. The mother cat was there too, and she purred when she saw Anna. Anna took hold of a kitten and carried it down the ladder. Then up she went again, and before long all six kittens were safely on the ground.

Then the little girl found an old basket, without a handle. She carefully put the kittens into it, and, with the mother cat trotting beside her, she went out of the barn and back to Mrs White's house.

How delighted Mrs White was to have her kittens back again, safe and sound! She was hunting for them everywhere!

'A dog came into the house and frightened the mother cat,' she told Anna. 'So I suppose she thought she had better take her kittens somewhere else. They would all have caught cold in that draughty barn. It *is* good of you to take so much trouble, Anna.'

'I love all animals,' said Anna, 'especially kittens. I'd love to have a pet of my own. Oh dear, look at my party dress! It's all dirty and I've torn it! I can't go to the party, I'm afraid!'

'Oh, I *am* sorry,' said Mrs White. 'Can't you go home and put another dress on?'

'I've only got my school dress besides this,' said Anna. 'It doesn't matter. I don't mind missing the party if I've rescued your kitten family! I do love them so much!'

So Anna missed the party, for she didn't want to go in her old school dress. She was very sad about it, and Mother was sorry for her. Mrs White had told Mother how kind Anna had been, so she understood all about it.

'Never mind, darling, you shall have an Easter egg,' said Mother, so Anna looked forward to that. She wondered if it would be a chocolate one. She did like chocolate very much.

There *was* a chocolate egg for her – and another egg, too – a most surprising Easter egg! Mother brought it into the dining room with such a funny smile on her face. It was an *enormous* cardboard egg, red, yellow and blue – and it made a noise!

It did really! And what sort of a noise do you think it made? Guess!

It *mewed*! Anna gave a scream of excitement and split the egg in half – and out jumped the dearest, prettiest little Persian kitten you ever saw! It was one that Anna had rescued from the barn that week!

'Mrs White said that you were just the right person to have one of her kittens,' said Mother. 'Do you like your Easter egg, Anna?'

'Mother, it's the loveliest one in all the world!' cried Anna. 'Oh, I don't mind missing the party if I have a kitten of my own. I am *so* happy!'

Wasn't it a surprising Easter egg?

Tick-a-Tock, the Greedy Rabbit

Tick-a-Tock, the
Greedy Rabbit

THERE WAS once a rabbit called Tick-a-Tock, who found three gold pieces lying in the sunshine. They shone and glittered, and Tick-a-Tock thought they were very beautiful.

'Now I am rich,' he said, and he felt very proud. He took the gold pieces to his burrow, and hid them there. Sometimes he took them out and counted them – one, two, three – three, two, one! And sometimes he counted them over and over again, until he came to the number one hundred and pretended he was very rich indeed.

'I won't spend them,' he said. 'If I do, I shan't be rich

any longer. I'll just keep them here to look at.'

Soon he began to wish that he had more than three. How exciting it would be if he had twelve to count! My! Wouldn't he be a rich rabbit!

'But how could I get some more?' he wondered. He thought and thought, and for a long time he couldn't think of any plan at all.

He was a silly rabbit, for he didn't need any money, not even a penny. He didn't have to pay for the grass he ate, nor for the tree bark he sharpened his teeth on, nor for the cosy burrow he lived in. He didn't have to pay for the sunshine that warmed him nor for the wind that cooled him. He just wanted the money to make him feel rich!

At last he thought of a good plan.

'I will do odd jobs for everyone,' he said. 'Then I will charge people a gold piece, and I shall soon have as many as I want.'

So he put up a notice outside his burrow which said:

ODD JOBS DONE.

APPLY INSIDE TODAY.

Then he waited for his customers to come.

Now many fairies lived round about Tick-a-Tock's home, and when they saw the rabbit's notice they were pleased. Tick-a-Tock hadn't a very good name for kindness, and the fairies all thought that he was turning over a new leaf, and was ready to do good turns to anyone. So the news soon went round that the rabbit would do all kinds of jobs – but nobody guessed that he meant to charge them gold pieces.

First of all Sammy Squirrel called on him, and begged him to act as postman for the day.

'I'm having a party,' he said, 'and there are so many invitations that I haven't time to take them all round myself, or I shall never get the jellies made.'

Tick-a-Tock jumped up at once, and took all the letters. He put them into his wallet, and started off. It didn't take him very long to deliver them, for a rabbit gets along very fast. The last invitation of all was one for himself, so he didn't have to deliver that. Then he went to Sammy Squirrel's.

'I've done your job,' he said. 'Now will you pay me, please?'

'Pay you!' said Sammy, looking most surprised. 'Whoever heard of paying for a kindly deed, I should like to know! We're not human beings, you know – we can afford to do things just out of kindness, which is much nicer! You must be mad, Tick-a-Tock!'

'No, I'm not,' said the rabbit. 'That will be one gold piece, please, Sammy. Come on, pay me quickly.'

'I haven't got even a silver piece,' said Sammy, crossly, 'and I shouldn't give it to you, if I had. I thought you were turning over a new leaf, and were going to do good turns to us all for a change. You've been a mean little rabbit for a long time!'

That made Tick-a-Tock furious, and he stamped off, tearing up his invitation as he went. He vowed he would make Sammy pay up some time or other.

Next day Fuff-Fuff the fairy went to ask him if he would carry a new dandelion clock from the hedge to her house, as her old clock was no use. She was such a tiny fairy that the weight was too much for her.

Well, that was nothing to Tick-a-Tock! He picked a fine dandelion clock, and in two minutes had taken it to where Fuff-Fuff lived in a red toadstool, and had stood it in her little hall.

'Oh, you kind rabbit!' she said, and kissed him on the nose.

'That little job will be one gold piece,' said Tick-a-Tock. Fuff-Fuff gave a scream, and then laughed.

'You must be having a joke!' she said. 'We don't expect to be paid for kind deeds in Fairyland.'

'Nonsense,' said Tick-a-Tock. 'One gold piece, please.'

Well, of course, Fuff-Fuff didn't give it to him. She simply shut her door in disgust, and wouldn't open it even when he banged twelve times on the knocker.

The next morning Tippity the elf came to Tick-a-Tock and begged him to carry him to his cousin Pippo, who was very ill.

'I've flown all through the night,' said poor Tippity, 'and I feel too tired to go any further. Then I saw your notice, so I came here to see if you could help me.'

In a trice Tick-a-Tock had galloped off to Pippo's with Tippity on his back. It only took ten minutes to take him there, and Tippity was very grateful.

'I'll never forget what you've done,' he said.

'Well, you must pay me a gold piece, please,' said Tick-a-Tock.

'Good gracious!' said Tippity, in dismay. 'Why, I thought you did these things for kindness.'

'No, certainly not,' said Tick-a-Tock.

He didn't get his gold piece from Tippity though, for the elf meant to spend all his money on his ill cousin, and he wouldn't give the greedy rabbit even a penny. He ran into Pippo's house and banged the door.

Then Tick-a-Tock began to make himself a dreadful nuisance. He went to Sammy Squirrel's every single day and shouted for his money. He went to Fuff-Fuff's too, and Tippity's, and made such a fuss and bother about his wretched gold pieces that at last the worried little things managed to get enough money together and give him a gold piece each. Tick-a-Tock was delighted, for now he had six gold pieces to count.

But the news soon went round that he charged for his kind deeds, and no one came to his burrow anymore. Then one day a dreadful thing happened to Tick-a-Tock.

He was running along through the wood when the wind was very high, and suddenly a tree came crashing down to the ground! Poor Tick-a-Tock was caught underneath one of the branches, and his leg was broken. He shouted for help, and who should come by but Sammy Squirrel!

Oh dear, oh dear, he won't help me, thought Tick-a-Tock. But he was quite mistaken. Sammy came running up and in two twinks he had lifted the branch and set Tick-a-Tock free.

'Half a minute,' he said. 'I'll get someone to help me carry you home.'

He ran off, and brought back Tippity the elf! Tick-a-Tock felt certain that Tippity wouldn't dream of helping him – but he did! He was dreadfully sorry about poor Tick-a-Tock's leg, and he and Sammy gently carried him home.

'You must have a nurse,' said Sammy, and he went to fetch one. Who should he bring back but Fuff-Fuff the fairy! Tick-a-Tock felt certain she wouldn't stay with him – but she did, and a very good little nurse she made! She brought his meals to him, and looked after him well until his leg had mended and he could go about once more.

'How much do you charge?' he asked Fuff-Fuff, when she said goodbye to him. 'Oh dear me, nothing at all,' she said. 'It's fine to do a kind deed, and I couldn't think of charging you anything, Tick-a-Tock!'

Sammy and Tippity said just the same thing, and Tick-a-Tock suddenly began to feel very ashamed of himself.

They might easily have charged me two gold pieces each! he thought. *I couldn't have said no, for they might have left me under that tree. Dear, dear, how very kind of them!*

The more he thought about things, the more ashamed he felt, and that night he got up and went to his store of gold pieces. He took three envelopes and put two pieces of gold into each. Then he ran to Sammy's and dropped one envelope into the letterbox. He did the same at Tippity's and Fuff-Fuff's, and then he went back home feeling very happy.

He didn't take down the notice outside his burrow. It is still there, and heaps of people go to him every day for help. For, you see, he doesn't charge anything at all now. He likes to do things for kindness, so no wonder he is the best loved rabbit in the whole of Fairyland. The queen heard of his good deeds and knighted him; so if ever you want his help, be sure to address your letters to Sir Tick-a-Tock Rabbit, or they might not reach him!

Jimmy and the
Jackdaw

Jimmy and the
Jackdaw

ONCE THERE was a boy called Jimmy. When he had a birthday his uncle gave him a book all about birds.

There were pictures of birds in it and pictures of birds' eggs too.

'Aren't they pretty?' Jimmy said to his friend Connie. 'Look at this picture of hedge sparrows' eggs – they are as blue as the sky. I've a good mind to look for a hedge sparrow's nest and take the eggs for myself.'

'Oh, you mustn't do that,' said Connie at once. 'It isn't kind to take the eggs out of a bird's nest. You know you mustn't do it.'

Jimmy didn't listen. It was springtime, and many

birds were building their nests. Jimmy saw them flying here and there with bits of straw or a feather in their beaks.

I shall look out for a hedge sparrow's nest and take the eggs, thought Jimmy. *I shall put the eggs into a box lined with cotton wool. No one will know.*

Well, he did find a hedge sparrow's nest. It was in the hawthorn hedge that ran beside the lane. Jimmy saw the bird fly into it, and he tiptoed to the hedge.

He parted the sprays and peeped into the heart of the hedge. At first he couldn't see the nest, and then suddenly he did. It was well tucked away, hidden by the green leaves.

And in the nest was the mother hedge sparrow, sitting on her eggs, keeping them warm! She looked at Jimmy, but she did not move.

'Fly away, fly away!' said Jimmy, and he shook the hedge. It was very unkind of him. The little brown bird was afraid. She flew up from her nest and perched on a nearby tree, watching anxiously.

Jimmy saw the pretty blue eggs there, four of them.

He was so greedy that he took them all. He did not leave the little mother bird even one.

She was very unhappy. She flew back to her nest after Jimmy had gone and looked sadly into it. Where were her pretty, very precious eggs? They were gone. The little hedge sparrow burst into a sad little song, and told the other birds around the dreadful thing that had so suddenly happened to her.

Jimmy went home with the eggs. They looked so very pretty on the white cotton wool in the box. They were so pretty that he thought he would like to draw and paint them. Jimmy was very, very good at drawing and painting.

'Now, where's my silver pencil?' said Jimmy. 'I can easily draw these eggs. I think I will draw a nest first and then draw the blue eggs inside.'

Jimmy began to draw with his silver pencil. He was very proud of that pencil, because he had won it at school as a drawing prize. No other boy had a silver pencil. Jimmy felt important when he took it out of his pocket at school to use it.

The next nest he found was a robin's. It was built on the ground under a hedge in Jimmy's own garden. There were four eggs in it, and Jimmy took them all. The robin made an angry clicking noise at him, but she couldn't stop him. She was very sad, and flew away from her nest, making up her mind that she would never build or sing in Jimmy's garden again.

Jimmy went on collecting eggs. He only told Connie about them, and wanted to show them to her, but she wouldn't look. 'I think you are bad and unkind,' she said. 'You are making a lot of birds unhappy. I don't like you.'

One day Jimmy walked by the old ruined castle. He heard the sound of many birds crying 'chack-chack-chack' and he looked up.

'What a lot of jackdaws!' he said to himself. 'Oh – wouldn't I like some jackdaws' eggs! I know I could find some if I climbed up to see.'

It wasn't very difficult for Jimmy to climb up to the castle tower. He found footholds in the crumbling stone, and made his way up little by little. Soon he found himself looking through a hole, inside which a jackdaw had built his enormous untidy nest of twigs.

And there, just within reach of Jimmy's hand, were three big eggs. 'What a bit of luck!' said Jimmy, and he put out his hand to take them.

Soon he was climbing down the walls again, the eggs safely in his pocket. He hurried home, and found a box big enough to put the eggs in. He really had quite a fine collection now! He took all the eggs every time he found a nest – he did not leave the mother bird even one or two. He did not think once of her sadness when she found she had no eggs left to sit on.

The next day Jimmy was sitting in his room by the open window, drawing a map of England for his geography lesson. He was using his lovely bright silver pencil, of course.

He got up to fetch his ruler, and put his pencil down on the window ledge. Just as he did this, a big bird, quite black except for a grey patch at the back of its head and neck, came flying by.

It was a jackdaw. It saw the silver pencil shining in the sun and it flew down to the sill at once. It loved bright, shiny things.

It picked the silver pencil up in its beak. It was heavy, but the jackdaw was a big, strong bird. Jimmy turned when he heard the flutter of wings.

He saw the jackdaw pick up his precious pencil. He saw him fly off with it in his beak! He saw him getting smaller and smaller as he flew right away to the castle tower, where he and the other jackdaws had their nests!

'Oh!' shouted Jimmy. 'Oh! You wicked bird! You've stolen my pencil! Come back, come back!'

But the jackdaw didn't come back. He put it into his nest. He already had a piece of silver paper there and somebody's shining thimble. The pencil looked nice laid beside them.

Jimmy was terribly upset. He ran to the window and yelled. He began to cry, and the tears ran down his cheeks like two little streams. He was still crying when Connie came into his room.

'That jackdaw is a thief!' wailed Jimmy. 'He has stolen my most precious thing – the silver pencil I loved.'

Connie looked at Jimmy, and didn't say anything.

'Why don't you say something?' cried Jimmy, wiping his tears. 'You know how much I loved my pencil. I won it for a prize. Aren't you sorry it's gone? It's most unfair of that jackdaw to come and take it like that.'

'Well, I think it was fair, not unfair,' said Connie, at last. 'After all, Jimmy, the jackdaw was doing exactly the same thing you did to him. You took his eggs – and he took your pencil.'

'But I loved my pencil!' cried Jimmy.

'Birds love their eggs,' said Connie. 'They wouldn't sit so long on them as they do, they wouldn't look so happy when they are sitting, if they didn't love their eggs, but you took them. The robin loved hers, and you took them. The jackdaw did too, but you took those.'

'But my pencil was made of silver and it was very

precious,' wept Jimmy.

'I expect birds' eggs are even more precious to them than your silver pencil was to you,' said Connie. 'After all, eggs have something alive in them – baby birds. I expect they are as precious to the bird as you are to your mother.'

'Connie, be nice to me, I am so unhappy,' said Jimmy.

'I would be nice to you if you could see that what has happened is quite fair and just,' said Connie. 'You said the jackdaw was wicked because he stole your pencil. Well, why can't you see that you were bad to steal his eggs? You do horrid things yourself – but you don't like it when the same kind of thing happens to you. And what is more, I don't think the jackdaw is wicked, because he doesn't know that stealing is wrong, and you do!'

'Oh, Connie, I do see that it's fair and just,' wept poor Jimmy. 'I do, I do. I won't take any more eggs. I was greedy and horrid to take every egg I saw. I won't do it anymore. I know what it's like now to be without something I love. Oh, I wish I hadn't been so horrid.'

Connie put her arms round him. "Don't cry,' she said. 'I'll be nice to you now you say that. Perhaps I could buy you a new pencil with the money out of my money box.'

'No, don't do that,' said Jimmy at once. 'Perhaps the jackdaw will bring my pencil back.'

But he didn't. It is still in his nest. Poor Jimmy! It was a hard punishment, but a very fair one, wasn't it?

First Walk in April

First Walk in April

April Showers

THE CHILDREN found out when Uncle Merry was due to come back, and they were all at the station to meet him. He was very pleased. As for Fergus, the little Scottie flung himself on them, barking madly, and then ran round and round them at top speed.

'Circus dog!' said Pat, with a laugh. 'Oh, it's nice to see you both again, Uncle Merry.'

'Well, it's good to see all of you too,' said Uncle Merry, taking his suitcase and leading the way out of the little station. 'I suppose you want me to keep my promise and take you for a nice long walk, straight away, now, this very minute, in fact, *at once!*'

The children laughed. 'We'll help you with your suitcase, and then you can come, can't you, if you're not tired? The country is lovely now. We've been for some walks by ourselves, Uncle, and we've spotted quite a lot of new flowers – *and* we've looked them up in our book – the one you lent us. We're longing to know if we are right.'

'Well, you really are bright children!' said Uncle Merry. 'I shall have to reward you. We'll go for a walk straight away – and as it is nearly dinnertime, we will take our meal with us and eat it somewhere sunny and warm. Can your mother manage sandwiches for everyone, do you think?'

'Oh yes – she's awfully good at that,' said Pat joyfully. 'I'll run on ahead and ask her.'

Before twenty minutes had passed, the five ramblers were on their way again, Pat carrying a kitbag full of sandwiches, biscuits and cake. It was a lovely day. The sky was as blue as cornflowers, and enormous white clouds sailed across it. 'Like heaps of cotton wool,' said John.

But there were showers as well as sunshine, for it was April. Mother had made them all take their mackintoshes, for sometimes the showers were very heavy. Uncle Merry had his too. Only Fergus was lucky enough not to need one.

'We'll show you the "new" flowers we have found, as we come to them,' said Pat. 'Look, there's one.'

He pointed to a plant with bright blue flowers growing on a nearby bank. 'Isn't it a glorious blue?' said Pat. 'The flowers look like eyes gazing at us, don't they?'

'One of its names is angel's eyes,' said Uncle Merry. 'Another name is bird's eye. It is another speedwell. You remember the little ivy-leaved speedwell we found earlier, don't you? Well, this is another of the same family, and its proper name is germander speedwell. Can you remember that – germander? You will certainly be able to remember its other names, they are so pretty.'

'Germander speedwell, bird's eye, angel's eye,' said

Janet. 'Lovely! I wish I had a set of names like that. Well, that's one new flower we found, Uncle. And there's another.'

The second one was a pure-white flower, whose five-petalled head was set on a very fine stalk, almost a thread. It had straight, brittle stems, hardly able to hold themselves upright.

'Isn't it dainty?' said Janet. 'What is it, Uncle Merry?'

'The stitchwort,' said Uncle Merry. 'Do you see its lovely orange-red stamens, Janet? It is called the stitchwort because of the fine stitch or thread on which the flower head hangs.'

'You do tell us interesting things,' said Janet, watching the dainty white flowers shake their heads on their fine 'stitches'. 'Now John – where's *your* new flower?'

'Oh, Uncle, I don't even know if it *is* a flower,' said John eagerly. 'It's the funniest thing you ever saw. First, when I saw it, it was a sort of twisted green sheath, growing straight upwards in the ditch. The next time I saw it the sheath thing was undoing itself, and then it looked like those things the old monks used to wear – hoods or cowls they were called, weren't they? And *then*, Uncle, a sort of poker grew straight up in the very middle of the sheath! What do you think of that?'

'*Most* extraordinary!' said Uncle Merry. 'Show me this poker-flower, will you?'

John took him to a nearby ditch, and showed him a curious plant. From big arrow-shaped, purple-blotched leaves rose a strange 'flower'. As John said, it was like a monk's cowl or hood in green, and in the middle was a purple 'poker', like a tall, round tongue.

'It's a bit like a tiny bulrush head, isn't it?' said Janet. 'Whatever is it, Uncle?'

'It's a wild arum,' said Uncle Merry, 'a very common wild plant, and a very strange and curious one. It has many names – lords and ladies, cuckoopint, wake-robin, and it grows freely everywhere. The lords are the purple pokers, the ladies are the paler ones you find.'

'It doesn't seem to have any stamens or stigmas at all,' said Pat, picking a wild arum and looking at the tongue or poker.

'It has plenty,' said Uncle Merry, and he stripped away the green sheath from the poker, and from below it too. The sheath bulged out there, and in the bulge grew stamens, stigmas and hairs. 'Look, two sorts of flowers, female and male,' said Uncle Merry, pointing to the stigmas and the stamens.

'There are some flies in this bottom part,' said Janet. 'What are they doing there?'

'Ah, there's quite a story to tell!' said Uncle Merry. 'This arum wants small flies to come and pollinate it. It wants pollen from another arum brought to its stigmas. So, to attract the kind of flies it wants, it sends out a nasty smell. Along come flies that like nasty smells, thinking there must be food for them somewhere, if there is a smell like that!'

'What do they do?' asked Pat.

'The flies creep into the sheath, and follow the smell downwards, past this bugle at the bottom of the poker,' said Uncle Merry. 'But alas for them – there is no nasty-smelling food down there to match the smell! They try to get out, but can't because the ring of hairs won't let them out. So they bustle about, cross and puzzled, and brush against these female flowers, the stigmas. They leave on the stigmas any pollen they have already got on their backs from other arums. Well, when the stigmas have the pollen they want to make berries, and the stamens have *their* turn.'

'*They* get ripe and send pollen over the flies, I suppose,' said Janet.

'They do,' said Uncle Merry; 'and then the arum kindly sends out some sweet nectar which the flies feast on. That is their reward. When they have feasted, the hairs allow them to creep out – and off they fly to another arum, ready to pollinate the next lot of stigmas, when they are once more imprisoned below the poker.'

'What a queer story!' said Janet, looking for more arums. 'Those little flies have quite exciting adventures! I shall think of them whenever I see lords and ladies now.'

'Come on,' said John, pulling at Uncle Merry's hand. 'Fergus is getting tired of waiting for us.'

So off they all went, chattering and laughing, keeping eyes and ears open for anything new and exciting. Janet was delighted to be with Uncle Merry again, and kept close by him, eager not to miss a word he said.

'Look at that blackthorn!' he suddenly said, pointing to a starry mass of blossom on the hedge nearby. 'Isn't it a fairy-like flower, set against the dark thorny twigs?'

'It's a bit like the hawthorn,' said Janet, stopping to look at it, 'only the hawthorn has red twigs, not black.'

'Yes,' said Uncle Merry, 'the hawthorn is the red thorn, and the sloe is the blackthorn; we shall find the little purple plums on the blackthorn in the autumn if we look for them!'

'Lots of the trees are leafing now,' cried Pat, pointing to the hedge, where bits of green were to be seen, and to the sheaf of twigs round the elm tree boles, all in tender green leaf. 'And look at the dear little leaves on the birch trees, Uncle. Isn't it a lovely time of year?'

'Do you notice the red elm tree flowers?' said Uncle Merry, pointing upwards. All the children looked, and, deep red against the blue April sky, they saw the masses of elm blossom. They were surprised.

'I never knew before that the elm tree had a flower,' said Janet. 'Have all trees got flowers, Uncle?'

'All of them,' said her uncle, 'the oak, the ash, the sycamore, the lime, as well as the laburnum, the apple, the hawthorn and all the rest. You must look for them this spring.'

'Look at the daisies, look at the daisies!' shouted John, who was in front with Fergus. He pointed to a grass bank, which was almost white with daisies. 'That bank looks as if it's sprinkled with snow!'

'If you can cover nine daisies with your foot, then it is springtime,' said Uncle Merry.

John tried and counted. 'Ten daisies!' he announced. 'So it's more than springtime! Hurrah!'

The sun suddenly went in as an enormous white cloud rushed across the sky. Big drops of rain pattered down, and the ramblers put on their mackintoshes quickly. 'Not enough to make us shelter,' said Uncle Merry, looking up. 'A real April shower – soon over! There – the sun is peeping out again already.'

'Where shall we have our dinner?' asked Pat. 'I'm hungry.'

'By the little stream that runs into and through the big pond at the side of the common,' said Uncle Merry. 'We may see a few water birds there.'

So, when they came to the chattering little stream, they found a lovely place under a willow tree whose fresh leaves shone golden in the sun, and sat down to enjoy their sandwiches. Fergus cuddled up by John, for he felt certain that the small boy would share nearly everything with him. And he was right!

A flash of brilliant blue shot down the stream by them and all three children cried out in wonder. 'What was that?'

'The kingfisher,' said Uncle Merry. 'Maybe he has

come to have his dinner with us! He is fond of perching on that branch there, overlooking the water. Ah – watch – here he is, back again – and on that very branch too. What luck! We may see him fishing for his dinner.'

The brilliant blue and green bird, his orange underparts glowing brightly, sat on the branch, watching the water. He had very little tail, which gave him rather a stumpy appearance, but his beak made up for that, for it was long and strong.

Suddenly he spied a fish in the stream, and dived head-first into the water. He was up again in a trice, a wriggling fish in his beak. A gulp – and it was gone!

In a few moments he dived in again – but this time he missed the fish. The children loved watching him as they sat by the waterside and ate their dinner.

Then a little black moorhen came up, her head bob-bob-bobbing as she swam over the water. When she saw the children she took fright, and disappeared below the water at once. The children laughed to see such a vanishing act.

'See her beak?' said Uncle Merry, pointing to a black speck moving across the surface of the water. 'She is swimming under the water, where you see those double wrinkles spreading out behind her on the stream. She probably has a nest somewhere, a big platform on the flattened rushes, where she lays her eggs. She always covers them carefully when she leaves.'

They finished their meal, cleared up the scraps so as to leave no litter anywhere, and went up the stream to the big pond. How the tadpoles had grown! Some of them had their back legs now, and they were very lively indeed. Minnows and sticklebacks swam in the sun-warmed water, and Uncle Merry made the children notice the spines on the stickleback.

'Do you see that little spined fish!' he asked. 'He builds a nest each spring, chases his mate in there to lay her eggs, and then keeps guard over them until they hatch.'

'I never before heard of a fish that made a nest!' said Janet, in amazement. 'What's it like?'

'Muff-like in shape,' said Uncle. 'Perhaps one day you will see one – you certainly would if you kept a pair of sticklebacks in an aquarium, and gave them bits and pieces to build a nest. Now I just want to show you the little creature I told you about that builds itself a house.'

Uncle Merry scraped about in the mud in a certain place in the pond – and brought up two curious creatures. He showed them to the children. It looked as if he was holding two tubes made of bits of stick and tiny grains.

'The little insect that lives inside these cases has a very soft body that other pond animals like to eat,' he said; 'so, to protect himself, he gathers together any odd bits and pieces he can find in the water, glues them together, and makes himself this funny little house. There he lives quite safely, putting out his head and legs when he wants to crawl about, and able to hide himself quickly when enemies swim near.'

'Do these funny little grubs turn into anything?' asked Janet.

'They are caddis grubs, the grubs of the caddis fly,' said Uncle Merry. 'There will come a day when they crawl from the water, and fly away into the air, complete with wings.'

The curious 'houses' were returned to the pond, and the children spent some time in watching the water snails on the weed, and some big black beetles coming up to the surface of the pond for air. The water was full of life, and the ramblers spent a whole hour watching the creatures that made it their home.

They didn't at all want to go home, but at last they had to. John found a robin's nest on the way back, in a very curious place. He saw an old boot lying in a ditch and when he went to look at it, there, inside it, was a robin's nest, with the bright-eyed robin sitting closely on it!

'What a funny place to build a nest!' said John, in delight. 'Look, everybody! The robin doesn't mind us seeing her a bit.'

'The robin loves to nest in anything that once belonged to her friend, Man,' said Uncle Merry. 'She will nest in old kettles and saucepans, in the pockets of scarecrows, and, as you see, even in a tramp's old boot.'

They went home through the water meadows, and exclaimed in delight at the sheet of gold they saw there. 'Kingcups!' cried Janet. 'Lovely golden marsh marigolds, Uncle! Aren't they beautiful? They belong to the buttercup family, surely – what did you call it now – Ranunculaceae?'

'Right,' said Uncle Merry. 'Yes – they are gorgeous flowers, aren't they? And look at that little pond over there, covered with white blossoms. They are another buttercup, a white one this time – the water crowfoot.

They all went to look at the sheet of little white water buttercups, the crowfoot. 'How funny!' said John, pulling at one of the plants. 'It's got two kinds of leaves. Uncle – this flat kind that floats on the surface of the water – and this stringy kind, all cut up, that grows in the water itself.'

'Each kind is needed by the crowfoot,' said Uncle Merry. 'It would be of no use to have flat leaves below the water, and no use to have stringy ones on top, for they wouldn't float.'

'Plants are very clever,' said John. 'Oh, Fergus – you've splashed me with mud. Uncle, he's trying to look for rabbits down that water vole's hole. Isn't he silly?'

Then home they all went, tired and happy, stopping only once more to pick a big bunch of the pale dog violets that grew by the hundred at the edge of the wood, and in sheltered places on the common. The gorse was ablaze there now, and was a magnificent sight. It sent out a glorious smell.

'Coconut!' said Janet.

'Vanilla!' said Pat.

'No – just lovely gorse, blazing in the hot April sun!' said Uncle Merry.

'That was one of the nicest walks we have ever had,' said John, remembering the robin's nest he had found, and the brilliant blue kingfisher. 'Wasn't that kingfisher lovely? I do wish he lived in my garden!'

The Magic Easter Egg

The Magic Easter Egg

THERE WAS once a chocolate shop in Fairyland, kept by old Mother Bottle. It was a most exciting shop. It had great big bottles full of sweets of all colours, wonderful boxes of chocolates, and candy, wrapped up in colourful paper.

But it was at Easter time that the shop was most colourful of all, for then Mother Bottle had so many Easter eggs she didn't know what to do.

And such glorious ones they were! Chocolate ones, marzipan ones, ones that broke themselves in half when you said 'Open, egg!' and showed you a surprise inside – perhaps a toy or a brooch. You can guess how all the fairies loved her shop.

One Easter her shop was more full of eggs than ever before, and all day fairies, brownies, gnomes and pixies looked longingly in at the window. They looked especially at one great big egg tied up with gold ribbon, right in the very middle of the window. It was a magic egg, and very expensive indeed.

Now Oll, the gnome, longed to buy that egg. So he counted out his gold, and he found he had twenty pieces. He tied them up in a bag and sat down to think.

'I don't believe that egg's more than twenty pieces of gold,' he said. 'But perhaps Mother Bottle wouldn't let me have it for that. The best thing to do would be to go into her shop when she is having lunch, leave the money on the counter and take the egg.'

So you can see by that, that he was not a very nice gnome. He ran off to the shop. It was just lunch-time. He peeped inside. No one was there. Mother Bottle was having her lunch.

Quickly, Oll slipped inside, put his moneybag on the counter, caught up the magic egg, and ran! The egg was very heavy, for it was half as big as Oll himself.

He panted and puffed all the way home, and when he got there he put the egg down on his table and looked at it proudly.

'I'll untie the ribbon and say "Open, egg",' he said, 'and see what happens! I might find all sorts of wonderful things inside!'

He untied the gold ribbon. 'Open, egg!' he cried in a loud voice.

Instantly the egg flew open, and out jumped a little imp! Oll looked just as scared as he could be. He never thought of anything like that at all.

'What can I do for you?' asked the imp, grinning. 'I am your servant.'

'Dear me, is that so?' said Oll, beginning to feel better. 'Well, well! Let me see! You can sweep my bedroom for me!'

The imp took a broom, leapt upstairs, and began sweeping.

Oll heard him. Swish! Swish! Swish!

'Well, that's very nice,' said Oll. 'Now I've got a servant who will do all my work!'

He settled himself in a cosy chair and began to read.

Swish! Swish! Swish! went the broom upstairs. Swish! Swish!

'He's doing it very thoroughly!' said Oll after a time. 'I'd better go and see if he's finished.'

He ran upstairs, but oh, my goodness! That imp had swept the bedroom nearly bare! He had swept up the chairs and pictures, stools and books, and now he was beginning to sweep them out of the window.

'Stop!' cried Oll. 'Stop! Whatever are you doing?'

'I can't stop working until you say the proper words!' said the imp, sweeping a chair out of the window. 'I'm magic!'

Well, Oll tried all the words he knew, but nothing he could think of stopped that imp.

'Perhaps you'd better tell me to do some other sort of work!' said the imp at last, when he had swept nearly everything out of the window or down the stairs. 'I can do any work you like, you know!'

'Dear, dear, I wish I'd known that before,' said Oll. 'Go into the garden and wash all my dusters, then.'

At once the imp ran downstairs, took a tub and water, and began to wash Oll's dirty dusters, while the gnome tried to put his bedroom straight.

Suddenly he heard shouts of laughter coming from the road outside, and looking out of the window, he saw a crowd of fairies and pixies leaning over his garden wall laughing.

It must be something that imp was doing! Oll rushed downstairs and out into the garden.

That imp had washed all the dusters and pegged them on the line, but he couldn't stop washing till he was told to do something else. So what do you think he had done?

He rushed indoors and fetched the tables and chairs, and washed those! Then he hung them on the line, and you can't think how silly they all looked! It was no wonder everyone was laughing. He was just going to peg up a lot of saucepans when Oll rushed out.

'Stop! Stop!' he cried.

'I can't!' said the imp, grinning. 'I'm magic! Think of something else for me to do!'

Well, would you believe it? Oll couldn't think of a single thing to tell the imp to do next! He just stood there, trying his hardest to think of something.

And then a dreadful thing happened.

The imp thought he would wash Oll next, and so he suddenly grabbed hold of him, put him in the tub and soaped him all over!

Splutter-splutter-splutter! went Oll, with soap in his mouth, eyes and nose. Splish-splash! 'Help! Help! Fetch Mother Bottle!' he shouted.

One of the watching fairies flew off, laughing, to fetch Mother Bottle. Poor Oll had the water squeezed out of him, and then the wicked imp began to peg him on the line to dry!

And that's where Mother Bottle found him when she came hurrying down the road! She laughed till the tears ran down her cheeks to see Oll among all the chairs and saucepans!

'I took your magic egg!' wept Oll. 'But I'm sorry. Tell your imp to stop! I don't know how to make him!'

'Easy enough!' said Mother Bottle. 'Go back to your egg!' she said to the imp.

Bang! Clap! He was gone, and through the open door Oll saw the split egg close together again. Mother Bottle unpegged him from the line.

'Well, you've been well punished for your dishonesty, Oll,' she said. 'You can have your gold back, unless you want to keep the egg. Do you?'

'No, no, no!' cried Oll. 'Take the magic egg away. That imp has turned my house upside-down, and made everyone laugh at me! Take the egg away!'

So Mother Bottle took the egg home, and left Oll to make his house tidy again. The egg was never seen in the window anymore, and what happened to it nobody knows. But people do say it will turn up again one day.

I'm sure I don't want it, though. Do you?

The Clock in the Wood

The Clock in the Wood

ONCE UPON a time three children went out to have a picnic. They were Bob, Mollie and Eileen. They had a basket full of nice things to eat and a ball to play with. They waved goodbye to their mother and set off to Bluebell Wood.

'Please start back at five o'cock,' she called to them. 'Uncle Jim will be here then and he will want to see you.'

'Yes, Mother,' called back the children. 'We've got our watches!'

They soon came to Bluebell Wood. It was a lovely placc. There were still some bluebells shining here and there like pools of blue water. The birds were singing in the trees, and the sunshine slanted through the green branches and made freckles of light on the grass below.

'Let's play hide-and-seek!' said Bob. 'We'll put the basket of tea things under this tree while we play. I'll hide my eyes first.'

When the others called 'Cuckoo', Bob ran to find them. He found Mollie – but as he ran after her he caught his foot in a tree root and over he went! He didn't hurt himself, but, oh, dear, he broke the glass of his watch!

'Look!' he said. 'My watch is broken! Isn't it a pity! Is yours all right, Mollie? We must know the time to go home.'

'Yes, mine's all right,' said Mollie. 'Never mind, Bob – we'll soon get yours mended!'

'What's the time, Mollie?' asked Eileen. 'Is it time for tea yet?'

'It's four o'clock,' said Mollie. 'Yes – we'd better have tea.' So they fetched their basket and handed out the good things – tomato sandwiches, chocolate cake and an apple each to eat. What a fine tea! There was nothing left at all except three paper bags and the milk bottle and cup when the children had finished!

'Let's have a game of catch now!' said Bob. So they began. It was great fun and they played for a long time. Then Bob wondered what the time was. He didn't want to miss seeing Uncle Jim! He looked at his watch. Oh, dear – it was broken! He had forgotten that. So he called to Mollie.

'Mollie, what's the time?' Mollie looked at her watch.

'Four o'clock!' she cried.

'But it can't be!' said Bob, surprised. 'You said it was four o'clock just before we had tea! Look again!'

Mollie looked – and then she held her watch up to her ear. 'Oh!' she cried in dismay. 'It's stopped. Now what shall we do? Eileen hasn't a watch! We can't tell the time!'

'I can!' said Eileen, suddenly. She ran to where a big dandelion plant grew and picked a big fluffy dandelion clock. She blew it hard. Puff! She blew again. Puff! Still there was some white fluff left. She blew again.

Puff! That was 1 o'clock, 2 o'clock, 3 o'clock – puff, 4 o'clock, puff, 5 o'clock!

'It's five o'clock!' cried Eileen. 'I've puffed all the fluff off. The dandelion clock says it's five o'clock – time to go home!'

'Come on then!' cried the others, and off they all went. Mother was so pleased to see them in such good time, for Uncle Jim had just come.

'It wasn't our watches that told us the right time!' said Eileen. 'It was the little clock in the wood, Uncle Jim!'

The Big Juicy
Carrot

The Big Juicy Carrot

ONE FINE morning, Bobtail, the rabbit, met Long-ears, the hare, and they set off together, talking about this and that.

They stopped by a hedge and lay quiet, for they could hear a cart passing. Bobtail peeped through and saw that it was a farm cart, laden with carrots and turnips. How his mouth watered!

And then, just as the cart passed where the two animals were crouching, a wheel ran over a great stone, and the jerk made a big, juicy, red carrot fall from the cart to the ground. The hare and the rabbit looked at it in great delight.

When the cart had gone out of sight the two of them hurried into the lane. Bobtail picked up the carrot. Long-ears spoke eagerly. 'We both saw it at once. We must share it!'

'Certainly!' said Bobtail. 'I will break it in half!'

So he broke the carrot in half – but although each piece measured the same, one bit was the thick top part of the carrot, and the other was the thin bottom part. Bobtail picked up the top part – but Long-ears stopped him.

'One piece is bigger than the other,' he said. 'There is no reason why *you* should have the bigger piece, cousin.'

'And no reason why *you* should, either!' said the rabbit crossly.

'Give it to me!' squealed the hare.

'Certainly *not*!' said the rabbit. They each glared at the other, but neither dared to do any more.

'We had better ask someone to judge between us,' said the hare, at last. 'Whom shall we ask?'

Bobtail looked all round, but he could see no

one but Neddy the donkey, peering over the hedge at them.

'There isn't anyone in sight except stupid old Neddy,' he said. 'It's not much good asking *him*. He has no brains to speak of!'

'That's true,' said Long-ears. 'He's an old stupid, everyone knows that. But who else is there to ask?'

'No one,' said Bobtail. 'Well, come on. Let's take the carrot to the donkey and ask him to choose which of us shall have the larger piece.'

So they ran through the hole in the hedge and went up to Neddy. He had heard every word they said and was not at all pleased to be thought so stupid.

The two creatures told him what they wanted.

'If I am so stupid as you think, I wonder you want me to judge,' said Neddy, blinking at them.

'Well, you will have to do,' said the rabbit. 'Now tell us – how are we to know which of us shall have the bigger piece?'

'I can soon put that right for you, even with *my* poor brain!' said Neddy. He took the larger piece in his mouth and bit off the end.

'Perhaps that will have made them the same size!' he said, crunching up the juicy bit of carrot he had bitten off.

But no – he had bitten off such a big piece that now the piece that *had* been the larger one was smaller than the other!

'Soon put *that* right!' said Neddy, and he picked up the second piece. He bit a large piece off that one, and then dropped it. But now it was much smaller than the first piece!

The hare and the rabbit watched in alarm. This was dreadful!

'Stop, Neddy!' said Long-ears. 'Give us what is left. You have no right to crunch up our carrot!'

'Well, I am only trying to help you!' said Neddy indignantly. 'Wait a moment. Perhaps *this* time I'll make the pieces equal.'

He took another bite at a piece of carrot – oh dear, such a big bite this time! The two animals were in despair.

'Give us the rest!' they begged. 'Do not eat any more!'

'Well,' said Neddy, looking at the last two juicy pieces, and keeping his foot on them so that the two animals could not get them, 'what about my payment for troubling to settle your quarrel? What will you give me for that?'

'Nothing at all!' cried Long-ears.

'What! Nothing at all?' said Neddy, in anger. 'Very well, then – I shall take my own payment!'

And with that he put his head down and took up the rest of the carrot! Chomp-chomp-chomp! He crunched it all up with great enjoyment.

'Thanks!' he said to Long-ears and Bobtail. 'That was very nice. I'm obliged to you.'

He cantered away to the other side of the field, and as he went, he brayed loudly with laughter. The two big-eyed creatures looked at one another.

'Bobtail,' said Long-ears, 'do you think that donkey was as stupid as we thought he was?'

'No, I don't,' groaned Bobtail. 'He was much

cleverer than we were – and you know, Long-ears, if one of us had been sensible, we would *both* now be nibbling carrot – instead of seeing that stupid donkey chewing it all up!'

They ran off – Bobtail to his hole and Long-ears to the field where he had his home. As for Neddy, he put his head over the wall and told his friend, the brown horse, all about that big juicy carrot.

You *should* have heard them laugh!

The Queer Little
Needles

The Queer Little Needles

KATIE WAS sitting on the floor with Roger. They had the ragbag between them and were pulling out all the bits and pieces. It was great fun.

'What are you looking for?' asked their mother.

'Well, I want a piece of silk to make Angeline, my doll, a new dress,' said Katie, 'and Roger wants a piece of blue velvet to make her a new coat. Her old coat is almost in rags.'

'Here's a fine piece of silk for Angeline's dress,' said Mother, picking up a piece of red silk. 'And here's just the thing for her coat – a beautiful piece of blue velvet. It was a bit that was left from your last years' party dress, Katie.'

The children were pleased. Katie cut the red silk into two halves to make a dress, and then she did her best to cut out Angeline's coat.

They threaded their needles, and began. But oh, it was difficult to sew the pieces together!

Roger pricked his finger at once and made it bleed. Katie's stitches were too big, but when she tried to do little ones, the red silk slipped about.

'Oh dear!' said Katie. 'Sewing is very difficult.'

'I wish my finger would stop bleeding,' said Roger, sucking it. 'It's making such a mess of the blue velvet.'

'Oh, I've pricked my thumb now!' cried poor Katie. So she had. She sat sucking her thumb and Roger sucked his finger. They looked very funny.

'Let's go out for a walk,' said Katie, as the sun shone into the room. 'I'm tired of sewing.'

So out they went, walking in the early spring sunshine, looking for primroses in the wood. And it was whilst they were hunting for primroses that they suddenly saw the funny old woman.

She was very small – only as tall as Katie, who was eight. She had a face like a little red apple and her eyes were as blue as Angeline's. When the children saw her she was kneeling down on the ground, hunting for something in the thick grass.

'Hello!' said Katie, stopping. 'What are you looking for? Can we help you?'

'Good morning,' said the apple-faced woman. 'Yes – do help me, please. I was taking a packet of yellow needles to Dame Sew-Sew, and I've dropped them all. It is so very difficult to find them in the grass.'

'We'll soon find them for you,' said Katie, and she and Roger kneeled down to pick up the queer little needles. They were all bright yellow, and were very sharp indeed. The funny thing was that they were sharp at both ends and were very difficult to pick up. The children soon pricked their fingers with them.

'If only I knew a little magic to get the needles together,' said the little woman. 'But I don't.'

'Well,' said Roger suddenly, his face going red with excitement, 'I've got something magic enough to get those needles out of the grass all together without us hunting like this for them.'

'Oh, what, Roger?' cried Katie, surprised. Roger put his hand into his pocket and brought out – his new magnet! You know what a magnet is, don't you? It is an odd thing shaped like a horseshoe, usually painted red at the top. It has strange powers, and Roger thought they were magic.

'Now,' he said. 'Watch the magic that my magnet can do!'

He put it down into the grass, holding it by the red middle – and at once all those little steel needles rushed to the magnet and clung to it! Yes, they really did! Not one hid itself in the grass any longer.

Roger lifted his magnet and showed the others all the needles clinging tightly to the two ends.

'There you are!' he said. 'What about my magic? Isn't it wonderful?'

'It is marvellous,' said the old woman, looking as if she couldn't believe it. 'Simply marvellous. What powerful magic you have!'

'Count the needles and see if they are all there,' said Katie. So the apple-faced woman counted each one. Yes, there were exactly fifty, the right number. She put them carefully into a bag.

'Thank you very much,' she said. 'I suppose you wouldn't give me that magic magnet, would you? I would so like to have it, to pick up all the needles I've lost about my house.'

'Yes, you can have it,' said Roger generously. He gave it to the old woman, and she was pleased as could be. 'I haven't much to give you in return,' she said, 'but if you like I could spare one of these needles. They are all magic, you know. You have only to stick one into anything you want sewn together, and say, 'Needle, sew! Needle, sew!' and it will sew beautifully, and make anything you want.'

'Oh,' said Katie in delight. 'That's just what we'd like. We're trying hard to make clothes for Angeline, but we do prick our fingers so.'

'Well, here you are,' said the old woman, and she took a small yellow needle from her bag. 'Now goodbye – I must hurry. Thank you so much for your magnet.'

She ran off – and Katie and Roger hurried home at top speed to try their magic needle. Won't it be fun for them to say, 'Needle, sew! Needle, sew!' and have all their toys' clothes made in a trice!

As for Roger's magic, you can try it yourself if you want to. Buy a little magnet and see it pick up all the needles on the table. You will be surprised!

The Big Box of
Chocolates

The Big Box of Chocolates

PETER PENNY had been very good to old Dame Twinkle when she had hurt her foot and couldn't go out to do her shopping. He had run her errands every morning for a week, and she was very grateful.

'I want to give you a present, Peter Penny,' she said. 'I wonder what you'd like. You have been very good to me.'

'I don't want anything, thank you,' said Peter Penny, who had been very well brought up and knew that it was wrong to expect presents for kindness.

'Well, I'm going to give you something,' said Dame Twinkle, who had also been well brought up and knew that she must certainly show Peter Penny how pleased she was with his kindness to her. 'How would you like that big box of chocolate animals that is in Mrs Peppermint's sweet shop?'

'Ooh!' said Peter Penny, his eyes opening wide. The big box of chocolate animals was perfectly lovely. All the little folk of the village had gone to look at it and had longed to have it. If Peter Penny had it he could give a party and his friends could all share the animals. It would be really lovely.

Dame Twinkle saw Peter's eyes shining brightly, so she at once went to Mrs Peppermint's shop and bought the box of chocolate animals. Then she gave it to Peter Penny with her love.

He had a large net bag with him, because he had to do his shopping that morning, so he thanked Dame Twinkle very much indeed, and put the box into his bag. Then off he went to do his shopping. He bought bacon and sausages, a pound of rice, a tin of cocoa, some flowers and a new saucepan. Everything was squashed into his big net bag and soon it felt very heavy.

Peter Penny went home through the Magic Wood. When he was halfway through, something dreadful happened. The bottom of his net bag broke into a hole, and out fell the big box of chocolate animals on to the soft grass. Peter Penny was swinging the bag as he went and singing a very loud and merry song, so he didn't know what had happened. The saucepan in the bag stopped anything else from falling out. Peter Penny went gaily on, not knowing at all that he had lost his precious box of chocolates.

Now not very far behind him came Mrs Twitter, who sold yellow canaries in her little shop. Always when she came through the Magic Wood she wished a wish, because sometimes wishes came true there. And today she wished her wish.

'I do wish I could find a nice present lying on the ground all waiting for me!' she wished.

And dear me, the very next moment what should she see on the ground but the big box of chocolate animals that Peter Penny had dropped! She gave a squeal of surprise and rushed at it in delight.

But when she saw what it was her eyes filled with tears. 'Chocolate!' she said. 'Oh dear, what a pity! Chocolate always makes me feel so sick. Whoever would have thought I'd find a box of chocolates when my wish came true!'

She picked up the box and carried it off. As she went she wondered what to do with it.

I know, she thought. *I'll give it to old Mr Ho-Ho. He's been ill in bed for a long time now, and I'm sure he would love to have a nice box of chocolate animals.*

So she went to Mr Ho-Ho's, and left the box with the little maid, who at once took it to Mr Ho-Ho.

He opened the box, and dear me, how his face fell when he saw what was inside.

'Chocolates!' he groaned. 'Would you believe it? Just what the doctor said I wasn't to have! What very bad luck! Oh bother, bother, bother!'

He lay and looked at them. Then he thought that it would be a very good idea to send the box to little Silvertip, the elf across the way. It was her birthday and he would like to send her something.

He knew she was very fond of chocolates.

So he sent his little maid with the big box across the way, and she knocked at the door. 'A present from Mr Ho-Ho,' she said when Silvertip opened the door. The little elf screamed with delight and ran indoors with it. But dear me, when she saw what it was, she sighed and sighed.

'Look!' she said to her elfin husband. 'Another box of chocolates! That makes the fifteenth I've had today for my birthday. Whatever shall I do?'

'Well, if you don't want it, don't waste it,' said her husband. 'Let me take it to Mother Hooky for her little boy. He'll love all these chocolate animals.'

'But he's such a very, very *naughty* little boy,' said Silvertip, who didn't like the small boy at all.

'Never mind,' said her husband. 'Naughty or good, he'll like chocolates.' So off he went and gave the box to Mother Hooky for Hoppy, her small brownie son.

She was pleased – but what a pity, when Hoppy came home from school he was so rude and naughty that she really could *not* give him the chocolates. She sent him straight to bed instead.

She sat and looked at the box. 'What shall I do with them?' she wondered. 'I can't eat chocolates myself, and if I leave them in the cupboard that naughty little boy will steal them. I know! I'll give them to that nice little Peter Penny. He has been so good to old Dame Twinkle lately, running all her errands for her, and I know he likes chocolates.'

So she went to Peter Penny's house. Nobody was in. There was no light anywhere. So Mother Hooky opened the kitchen window and popped the box on the table just inside. She smiled to herself and thought, *I won't tell Peter Penny what I've done. He can just find them and wonder where they've come from!*

Now when Peter Penny had got home that morning, he had emptied his net bag on the table and looked for the box of chocolates at once. He thought he would like to eat one of the chocolate bears. They did look so very nice.

But to his great disappointment and horror there was no box there! It was gone. Then he saw the big hole in the bottom of the bag and he guessed what had happened. How upset he was!

'What bad luck!' he said to himself. 'To lose that wonderful box of chocolates – the best one I've ever had in all my life! Oh dear, I suppose I must go all the way back through the wood to see where I've dropped it.'

Poor Peter Penny! He had his dinner and then off he went to see if he could find his lovely box of chocolates. He looked here and he looked there, he hunted in the wood, he hunted in the fields. But no matter how hard he looked there was no box of chocolates to be seen. It was quite gone.

Peter Penny was tired and miserable. He couldn't help a few tears squeezing out on to his cheeks as he went home. He was very nearly home when he met Smarty the gnome, who thought himself very clever indeed.

'What's the matter, Peter Penny?' asked Smarty, staring at Peter's tears in surprise.

'Oh, nothing,' said Peter.

'Tell me what's the matter,' said Smarty, who was always curious to know everybody's business. 'Has someone been teasing you?'

'Of course not!' said Peter, crossly. 'Do you suppose I'd be so feeble as to cry if somebody teased me?'

'Well, what's the matter, then?' asked Smarty, simply longing to know.

So Peter Penny told him all about how he had been kind to Dame Twinkle, and how she had given him the wonderful box of chocolates, and how he had lost them.

'It's the first reward I've ever had for being kind,' said Peter, sadly, 'and now I've lost it.'

'Oh, that's the way of the world,' said Smarty, at once. 'It doesn't pay to be kind, you know, because you hardly ever get anything back for it, and if you do, you're bound to lose it. No, my boy, you listen to my advice. Don't go bothering to do kind deeds. Just get what you can out of other people, and look after yourself! It doesn't *pay* to be kind and good.'

'It certainly doesn't seem to,' said Peter Penny. 'It's

very hard to lose that lovely box of chocolates. I shan't bother to be kind to anyone again.'

He said goodbye to Smarty and went on. He hadn't gone very far when he saw old Mister Candleshoe, almost bent double under a big load of wood. Now Peter was really a very kind little fellow and his first thought was to go and help Mister Candleshoe.

Then he stopped himself. *No*, he thought, *I won't. Why should I help him? I shan't get anything out of it. As Smarty says, kindness doesn't pay.*

So he went right past Mister Candleshoe, and didn't even say 'good afternoon'.

But no sooner had he passed him than Peter Penny felt bitterly ashamed of himself and he went as red as a sunset sky. *How horrid of me!* he thought. *Am I so mean that I can't give a hand to an old chap like Candleshoe? What do I care if kindness is rewarded or not? I shall be kind because I want to be!*

So back he went and took Candleshoe's big bundle away from him. He carried it all the way home for him and then turned to go to his own cottage.

'You're a kindly fellow!' called Candleshoe after him. 'A rare, kindly fellow, you are, Peter Penny. May you get what you most want today!'

Peter Penny smiled a crooked little smile. *What I most want is that perfectly lovely box of chocolate animals*, he thought. *But that's gone for good.*

Then he stopped in the greatest astonishment, for there, set on the kitchen table, was the very box of chocolates he had lost that morning. There it was, with no note, no message. How did it get there? Where did it come from? What a very extraordinary thing!

'Ooh!' said Peter Penny, in delight, picking it up. 'Ooh! Who says kindness isn't rewarded!'

He danced round and round the room in joy, and a chocolate bear fell out of the box. Peter Penny picked it up and ate it. It was delicious.

'Now to write out the invitations to my chocolate party!' cried the little fellow, happily. 'What fun we shall have!'

And when all his friends came to the party Peter Penny told them about the very mysterious way in which the box of chocolate animals had appeared in his kitchen, and they were really most astonished.

'You deserve all the good luck you get,' said his friends, hugging him. I think he does too, don't you?

The Blown-Away Rabbit

The Blown-Away
Rabbit

THERE WAS once a small rabbit who was a very friendly creature. His name was Bobbin, and if you could have seen his white tail bobbing up and down as he ran, you would have thought this name was a very good one!

He lived just outside the farmyard, near the pond where the big white ducks lived. He used to play with the yellow ducklings, and they were very fond of him.

One day Waggle-Tail, the smallest duck, had a terrible fright. He ran away from the others, because he wanted to see if there was a puddle he could swim on all by himself. The pond seemed so crowded when all the white ducks and the yellow ducklings were on it.

Well, Waggle-Tail waddled off to where he saw the rain puddle shining. It was a very nice puddle indeed. Waggle-Tail sat on it and did a little swim all round it, quacking in his small duckling voice.

The farm cat heard him, and left his seat on the wall at once. Young fat ducklings made wonderful dinners for cats – but usually the ducklings kept with the big ducks, and the farm cat was afraid then.

'A duckling on a puddle by itself!' said the big grey cat to himself in joy. He crept round by the wall. He crept round the pigsty. He crouched low and waggled his body ready to jump – and just then the duckling saw him. With a terrified quack he scrambled off the puddle and ran to find his mother.

But he went the wrong way, poor little thing. He went under the field gate instead of under the gate that led to the pond. The cat crept after him, his tail swinging from side to side.

'Quack! Quack! Quack!' cried the yellow duckling.

'Quack! Quack! Quack!'

But his mother didn't hear him. Nobody heard him – but wait! Yes – somebody *has* heard him! It is Bobbin the little rabbit!

Bobbin heard the duckling's quacking, and popped his long ears out of his burrow. He saw Waggle-Tail waddling along – and he saw the farm cat after him.

'Waggle-Tail, Waggle-Tail, get into my burrow, quickly!' cried Bobbin. Waggle-Tail heard him and waddled to the burrow. The cat would have caught him before he got there, if Bobbin hadn't leapt out and jumped right over the cat, giving him such a fright that he stopped for just a moment.

And in that moment the little duckling was able to run into the rabbit's hole! Down the dark burrow he waddled, quacking loudly, giving all the rabbits there *such* a surprise!

Bobbin leapt into the hole too, and the friends sat side by side, wondering if the cat was still outside.

'I daren't go out, I daren't go out,' quacked poor Waggle-Tail.

'I will go and fetch your big white mother duck,' said Bobbin. 'I can go out to the pond by the hole that leads there. Stay here for a little while.'

Bobbin ran down another hole and up a burrow that led to the bank of the pond. He popped out his furry head and called to Waggle-Tail's mother.

'That cat nearly caught Waggle-Tail. He is down my burrow. Please will you come and fetch him.'

So the big white duck waddled from the pond and went to fetch her duckling from Bobbin's burrow. She was very grateful indeed to Bobbin for saving her little Waggle-Tail.

'Maybe some day I shall be able to do you a good turn too,' she said. And off she went, quacking loudly and fiercely at the farm cat, who was now lying in the sun on the wall.

Now not long after that, Bobbin wanted to go and see Waggle-Tail – but when he put his nose out of the burrow he found that it was raining very hard indeed.

'You must not go out in that rain,' said his mother. 'Your nice fur will be soaked. Wait till it stops.'

But it didn't stop. The rain went on and on and on. Bobbin was very cross. *I will borrow an umbrella*, he thought. So he went to his Great-Aunt Jemima, and was just going to ask her for an umbrella when he saw that she was fast asleep, with her paws folded in her shawl. But there was the big red-and-green umbrella standing in the corner!

Bobbin knew that no one should borrow things without asking, but he simply couldn't wait until Aunt Jemima woke up. So the little rabbit tiptoed to the corner and took the big old umbrella.

He scuttled up the burrow with it, dragging it behind him. He pulled it out of the hole and put it up. My goodness, it *was* a big one!

Bobbin held on to the big crook handle and set off down the hillside. It was a very windy day, and the big purple clouds slid swiftly across the sky. A great gust of wind came, took hold of the umbrella – and blew it up into the sky!

And Bobbin went with it! He was such a little rabbit that the wind swept him right off his feet with the umbrella – and there he was, flying along in the sky, holding on to the umbrella!

He was dreadfully frightened. He clung to the handle with his two paws, hoping that he wouldn't fall, but feeling quite sure that he would, very soon. Poor Bobbin!

The wind swept him right over the pond. The ducklings looked up in surprise when they saw the enormous umbrella – but how they stared when they saw poor Bobbin hanging on to it too!

'It's a rabbit, it's a rabbit!' they cried.

And Waggle-Tail knew which rabbit it was. 'It's Bobbin, my dear friend Bobbin!' quacked Waggle-Tail. 'Mother, Mother, look at Bobbin! He will fall. What can we do to save Bobbin? He saved *me* – we must save *him*!'

'But how can we?' said the mother duck.

'Mother, can't you fly after him?' cried Waggle-Tail. 'I know you don't often fly, because you prefer to swim – but couldn't you just try to fly after poor Bobbin?'

'I will try,' said the big mother duck. So she spread

her big white wings and rose into the air. She flapped her wings and flew after the big umbrella. Bobbin was still holding on, but his paws were getting so tired that he knew he would have to fall very soon.

The mother duck flew faster and faster on her great wings. She caught up the umbrella. She flew under the surprised rabbit and quacked to him.

'Sit on my back! Sit on my back!'

Bobbin saw her just below him. He let go the umbrella handle and fell neatly on to the duck's broad, soft back – plop! He held on to her feathers.

Down to the pond she went, carrying the frightened rabbit. What a welcome the little ducklings gave him! As for Waggle-Tail, he could hardly stop quacking!

'You did me a good turn, and now my mother has paid it back!' he quacked 'Oh, I'm so glad you're safe!'

'So am I,' said Bobbin. 'But, oh dear, what about my Aunt Jemima's umbrella? It's gone to the clouds!'

It came down again the next day, and fell into the field where Neddy the donkey lived. Neddy took the handle into his mouth and trotted to Bobbin's burrow with it.

'Here you are!' he said to Bobbin. 'I heard that your Aunt Jemima might smack you for taking her umbrella without asking. I hope she hasn't.'

'No, she hasn't,' said Bobbin joyfully. 'Oh, thank you, Neddy! What good friends I have!'

He ran down the burrow with the big umbrella, meaning to give it to his Great-Aunt Jemima. But she was asleep again, with her paws folded in her shawl, so Bobbin quietly stood the umbrella in the corner and ran off to tell Waggle-Tail.

'Don't get blown away again, will you, Bobbin?' begged the duckling. And Bobbin promised that he wouldn't. He didn't want any more adventures just then!

The Top of the
Wall

The Top of the Wall

OLD MAN Greeneyes lived in a little cottage surrounded on all sides by a high red wall. He liked to be sheltered from the winds – and from prying eyes; for Old Man Greeneyes was half a wizard!

Next door to him lived Dame Fiddlesticks and her children. Dame Fiddlesticks was a most inquisitive person and loved to peep at her neighbours. If she went into her bedroom she could just see nicely over the wall into the old man's garden. That *did* annoy him! And then the children took to climbing on the top of the wall and calling to him. That annoyed him more than ever!

At last he decided that he must do something about it. If he had the wall made higher by a foot, and put some glass spikes on top, Dame Fiddlesticks couldn't see into his garden from her bedroom window and the children wouldn't be able to climb up and sit on top. So off he went to Mr Hod the builder.

'Yes,' said Mr Hod. 'It would be easy to do what you want – but you will offend Dame Fiddlesticks mightily. She might throw her rubbish over your wall in revenge, and her children would certainly call out after you when you go walking, for they are not very well-mannered. Take my advice and think of something else. It is usually just as possible to get your way in a kindly manner as in an ill-natured one.'

Old Man Greeneyes nodded his head and went to see his cousin, Mother Tiptap. She heard what he had to say and smiled. 'I've just the thing for you!' she said. 'See, here are some new seeds I have made. Plant them on the top of your wall and see what happens.'

'But no seeds will grow on a *wall*,' said Old Man Greeneyes. Still, he took them and planted them all along the top of his wall. Then he waited to see what would happen. The rain came. The sun shone. Those tiny seeds thrust out roots into the wall-crannies. They sent up small leaves. They grew and they grew.

And then one day in the springtime they flowered into bright yellow and red – tall plants, over a foot high, with the most delicious scent in the world! Old Man Greeneyes smelt them from his kitchen window and was glad. Dame Fiddlesticks feasted her eyes on them, for she loved flowers, and when she smelt their scent she was full of joy.

'Don't you dare to climb up on that wall anymore!' she warned her children. 'I won't have those beautiful flowers spoilt that that kind old man has planted there. They've grown so high that I can't peep into his garden anymore, but what does that matter? I'd rather see the flowers there!'

She was so delighted that she sent in a new cake she had baked to the old man. He went to thank her and asked what he could do in return for her kindness.

'Oh, if only you'd give me a few seeds of those

lovely flowers of yours growing on the wall,' she said. 'What are they called?'

'They've no name at present,' said the old man, smiling. 'What shall we call them? Let's ask the children.'

The children knew what to call them, of course! Do *you* know the name?

Fairy Easter Eggs

Fairy Easter Eggs

ONCE UPON a time there lived an uncle and aunt who didn't believe in fairies. They lived on the edge of a wood, and though Ben and Mary, their nephew and niece, knew perfectly well that the wood was simply *full* of fairy folk, Uncle John and Aunt Judy said it was all nonsense.

'But we *saw* two little gnomes only yesterday,' said Ben. 'Truly, Uncle. They were running by the hazel trees.'

'Stuff and rubbish!' said Uncle John.

'And, Auntie, I played with a fairy all yesterday morning!' said Mary.

'Fiddlesticks!' said Aunt Judy, who was busy cooking. 'Don't tell stories.'

Ben and Mary said no more. They ran off into the garden and began to play. If only Uncle John and Aunt Judy had believed in fairies, they would have been quite happy. Hollyhock Cottage was a jolly place to live in, and there were lots of chickens to feed and flowers to pick.

Sometimes Ben and Mary fed the hens themselves, and they always fetched in the eggs. Aunt Judy let them have a new-laid egg every morning for breakfast. She used to choose the brownest eggs for them because she thought they tasted the nicest of any.

So you see Aunt Judy was really very kind.

'If *only* she wouldn't keep saying there aren't any fairies,' sighed Mary. 'Even if she's never seen one herself, that doesn't *prove* there aren't any!'

'Of course it doesn't,' said Ben. 'And if Uncle John knew how often he nearly catches a fairy when he chases butterflies and moths for his collection, he *would* be surprised!'

'Let's go and tell the fairies about it,' suggested Mary. 'We've got nothing else to do, and there's half an hour before tea.'

Off they ran into the wood. When they came to a little sunken dell, they sat down beneath some hazel trees. No fairies were about, it seemed, but Ben and Mary knew that the Little Folk only come when mortals are quiet and peaceful.

They kept a sharp lookout, and presently Mary spied one peeping from beneath some violet leaves. Then Ben saw one dressed in grey, swinging on the pussy willow, and soon, as the children kept quite still, a score more little peeping heads showed from behind toadstools and tree trunks.

'It's only Ben and Mary!' cried a shrill little voice suddenly, and the pussy willow fairy flew down beside the children. Then out ran a dozen others, and down flew more still, until a chattering, skipping little group surrounded Ben and Mary.

'Why didn't you come and play yesterday?'

'Why didn't you come earlier today?'

'Why do you look unhappy?'

The fairies called out their questions in little high voices, and some of them climbed on to Mary's knee.

'We're not *really* unhappy,' said Mary. 'But you see, Uncle and Aunt don't believe in fairies, and they say we tell stories about you.'

'And that makes us sad, of course,' said Ben, 'because we *don't* tell stories about you or anything else. We always talk truly, don't we, Mary?'

'Couldn't you somehow or other make Uncle or Auntie know about you?' asked Mary. 'Couldn't you all suddenly fly into Auntie's kitchen or something?'

Ben giggled. 'That *would* give her a surprise!' he chuckled. 'Or couldn't you take turns at sliding down Uncle's newspaper in the mornings?'

The fairies shook their heads. 'We're not allowed to show ourselves to people who don't believe in us,' they answered.

'Oh, please,' begged Mary. 'Please! Remember how we helped you to find those two little lost fairies last summer, and how often we have brought you honey from our beehive.'

The pussy willow fairy put his hands in his pockets, and began to speak.

'I was one of those lost fairies,' he said. 'I don't mind helping you if someone else will join me.'

Another little fairy crept from behind a daffodil, where she had been listening to all that went on.

'I was the other lost fairy,' she said in a tiny little voice. 'I'll help you too.'

'Splendid!' said Ben in delight. 'Now the thing is – what shall we do?'

'They ought to hide somewhere and then suddenly fly out when Auntie and Uncle are near,' said Mary.

'Yes – something like that!' said Ben. 'Let's think hard!'

Everybody thought for two minutes.

Then Ben suddenly lifted his head and smiled.

'Could you get inside an egg?' he asked the willow fairy.

'Easily,' answered the fairy in astonishment.

'Well, listen!' cried Ben. 'We have the two brownest eggs every morning for breakfast. Can you by magic get inside the two brown eggs we'll have, so that when we crack them in the morning we'll find you there curled up, alive and real?'

'Oh, *then* we could show you to Auntie and Uncle, and they'd know!' cried Mary. 'They'd know it was magic too, to get inside an *egg*!'

'We can make two very brown eggs by using a spell,' said the willow fairy, slowly. 'But if we get inside them and ask the other fairies to carry us to your hen's nest, will you promise that no harm shall come to us tomorrow morning, when you have opened the eggs?'

'Yes, yes, we promise you!' cried Ben and Mary gladly. 'Will you do it then?'

'Yes, we will,' answered the two fairies. 'We'll be there tonight in the two brownest eggs. Carry us carefully when you take us in!'

The two children ran off feeling most excited. Aunt Judy and Uncle John would soon believe in fairies!

They were just in time for tea. They said nothing of where they had been, but they longed for the time to come when Aunt Judy would send them out to bring in any eggs laid since the morning.

'Just run and bring in the eggs,' she said at last.

Off the children ran. They raced down the path to the henhouse, and lifted up the lids of the nesting boxes.

'One, two, three, four, five, six, seven eggs, Mary!' cried Ben. 'And look at these two brown ones! They must be the magic ones. How exciting!'

'You'd better carry those two, Ben,' said Mary nervously. 'I'll carry the others. *Do* be careful of the fairy eggs.'

Ben was tremendously careful of them. He carried one in each hand, and walked slowly up the path to the kitchen door.

He put the eggs in a basket on the table, and Mary carefully put the others in, too.

'Seven eggs, Auntie,' she said, in rather a shaky voice, 'and two of them are *very* brown.'

'You shall have those for breakfast, then,' said Aunt Judy. 'Now run away. I'm going to be busy.'

Off they went, full of excitement, to think of what would happen next morning.

But they had forgotten that the next day was Easter Sunday.

Aunt Judy had bought two fine chocolate Easter eggs for them, and as she looked at the hens' eggs that the children had brought in an idea came to her.

'I'll paint all the eggs for tomorrow's breakfast just as my mother used to do when *I* was a child!' she decided. 'There's something very exciting about coloured eggs on Easter Sunday! Let me see – two for Uncle John, one for Ben, one for Mary, and one for me! What fun it will be!'

She quickly got her cochineal out of the cupboard to make the eggs red. Then she decided that it would make them look very gay if she used Uncle John's purple ink and some of his green ink. She fetched them.

The eggs began to look so gay! They had red at the

top and bottom, stripes of green and crosses of purple here and there.

'Won't Ben and Mary be pleased!' chuckled Aunt Judy, and put them carefully on a shelf to dry.

'But, dear me!' she said, as she stood looking at them. 'They're so gay with colours that I really can't tell which were the two brown ones I promised Ben and Mary! Never mind, it won't matter for once!'

Next morning the two children ran hurriedly downstairs to breakfast.

'Come along, dears,' said Aunt Judy, 'your eggs are all ready.'

Ben and Mary looked at their plates – then they looked again – then they rubbed their eyes and stared hard.

'What's happened to the eggs, Auntie?' asked Mary at last in an astonished voice.

Aunt Judy laughed at their surprise, and began to pour out tea.

'It's Easter Sunday, so I thought you should have gay Easter eggs!' she said. 'They're all painted, look!'

Ben and Mary saw that their uncle's and aunt's eggs were just as gay, and they began to feel relieved.

'I thought some of the magic had gone wrong,' Mary whispered to Ben.

'Eat your eggs, children,' said Aunt Judy, opening her letters.

'Now for it!' whispered Ben. He took his spoon and Mary took hers.

Crack-a-crack-crack!

They gently tapped the eggshell and cracked it. They took it off and laid it on their plates.

Then they stared at each other in the greatest disappointment and astonishment, for the eggs were proper ones, with white and yolk – no fairies were there at all!

Tears came into Mary's eyes, and Ben looked gloomy.

'The fairies must have been afraid at the last minute,' he said to his sister. 'Cheer up, Mary, and eat your egg. We'll think of another idea.'

Just then Uncle John began to crack *his* egg. He

took off the shell top and peered in surprise. He felt for his glasses and put them on his nose. Then he stared again at his egg.

'Judy, my dear,' he said at last to his wife.

'What, John?' asked Aunt Judy.

'This egg's *bad*,' said Uncle John.

'Dear, dear, dear, but it *can't* be,' said Aunt Judy. 'Why, it was only laid yesterday.'

'Well, there's nothing in it except a little mess at the bottom,' said Uncle John in disgust.

Then an astonishing thing happened. Out of the egg flew a tiny fairy, and shrieked at Uncle John in an angry voice.

'I'm *not* a little mess, I'm *not* a little mess!'

Uncle John started back in astonishment.

'Bless my buttons!' he cried. 'It's a squeaking butterfly! I must catch it for my collection!'

Directly the fairy heard that she gave a cry of fright and flew straight out of the window.

Ben and Mary sat watching in the greatest astonishment.

'The eggs have got mixed!' suddenly wailed Mary.

'Mixed! What do you mean, *mixed*?' asked Aunt Judy, who was lost in amazement at the sight of something flying out of one of her new-laid eggs.

'Oh, Auntie, I'll show you!' said Ben. 'Please will you let me crack the other two eggs that are left?'

'And Uncle, *darling*,' said Mary, 'please put that horrid net away for just a minute.'

Uncle John, thoroughly puzzled, let it fall on to the floor.

Then Ben carefully cracked one of the remaining two eggs. No, it was a proper one. He reached for the other.

Crack-a-crack!

It was a fairy egg!

Down at the bottom lay the little pussy willow fairy curled up tightly, looking at Ben with wide frightened eyes.

'My goodness gracious!' sighed Aunt Judy, her face flushing red with astonishment and delight. 'Did ever you see such a beautiful wee creature! What is it?'

'A fairy!' said Ben. 'Look, Uncle!'

Uncle John stared hard into the egg. He was very short-sighted, so perhaps that explains his mistake.

'Call it a fairy or anything you like,' he said. '*I* call it a butterfly, and how it got inside that egg is a marvel and a mystery to me. But if you're set on its being a fairy, I won't say anything more! Your eyes are better than mine!'

He picked up his net to put it away. But the fairy thought he was going to catch him, and he flew straight up in fright just as Uncle John bent over the egg once more.

Bump he went into Uncle John's nose, and sent his glasses clattering on to the table! Then out of the window he flew, and disappeared among the trees outside.

'That was a very *solid* butterfly, anyway!' said Uncle John, in surprise.

Aunt Judy didn't say much. She just ate her rolls and honey, and thought. Ben and Mary didn't dare to say anything either. As for Uncle John, he kept wondering out loud all breakfast what sort of butterflies those 'egg things' were.

But after breakfast Aunt Judy called Ben and Mary to her, and gave them the lovely chocolate eggs she had bought for them.

'Here you are,' she said, 'take them out into the wood and play with the fairies.'

So you see they *knew* she believed in them from that very morning, and they ran off as happy as could be.

But you *should* just have heard the fairies storming because one of them had been called a 'little mess', and both had been called butterflies! It took Ben and Mary a long time to make them pleased again.

And then how they laughed to hear that the pussy willow fairy had bumped Uncle John's spectacles off!

Goosey-Goosey Gander

Goosey-Goosey Gander

THERE WAS once a large grey gander who belonged to Mrs Tubby and her husband. He was very clever and, really, he almost understood what Mrs Tubby used to say to him each day.

'Goosey Gander follows me about like a dog,' said Mrs Tubby, proudly. 'And see, husband, he can shut the gate with his beak just as easily as I shut it with my hand!'

Sure enough the goose could shut the gate. He had watched Mrs Tubby shut the field gate every day, and he knew exactly how to slip the catch in its place. He really was a very clever bird.

Mr Tubby was a shepherd, and looked after the sheep and the lambs on Farmer Giles's hillside. He hadn't very much money, but he grew potatoes and cabbages in his little garden, and they made quite good soup when Mrs Tubby had cooked them in her own special way.

One day Mrs Tubby slipped on the kitchen floor and twisted her ankle. Mr Tubby fetched the doctor, and he shook his head gravely.

'Dear, dear!' he said. 'This is serious, Mrs Tubby. You will have to go to bed until your ankle is better. I will come and see you every day.'

Poor Mrs Tubby! There was such a lot to do in the cottage and only her to do it, for Mr Tubby was minding sheep all day. He wondered how they were going to manage, and then he went to fetch his little niece, Mary. She was only nine years old, but she was a very useful little girl.

'Yes, Uncle Tubby,' she said, 'I will come and look after Aunt Tubby till she is well. I can cook dinner and I can do housework. Don't worry.'

So Mr Tubby didn't worry anymore, but left things to Mary. She made the beds, washed up, cooked and scrubbed, and was the most useful little girl in the world. She fed Goosey Gander too, and he was very fond of her. She always left him to shut the gate of the sheep field when she took Uncle Tubby his dinner, and he never forgot.

When Mrs Tubby was better, and Mary had gone back home, Mr Tubby began to worry about the doctor's bill.

'How can we pay it?' he said. 'It isn't much, it's true, because he's only charged us a sixpence a visit but I haven't any money put by, wife.'

'We must sell the old Goosey Gander,' said Mrs Tubby. 'He's the only thing we've got that will fetch money.'

'Well, I'll be sorry to part with him,' said Mr Tubby, with a sigh. 'He's a good bird, and great company. He often comes and sits with me when I'm minding my sheep. Still, the doctor's bill must be paid, so he must go.'

Poor Goosey Gander! He was very much upset when Mrs Tubby told him he was to go to market and be sold. He was afraid that he might be fattened up and eaten for somebody's Christmas dinner. He worried about it so much that it kept him awake at night.

One moonlight night when Goosey Gander was sitting on one leg in the little shed, wide awake and sad, he heard a noise. He waddled to the door and looked out. The moon was up and shone down brightly. Goosey Gander looked up the hillside, trying to see if the sheep and lambs were safe.

And what did he see but a dark figure going in at the sheep field gate! It wasn't Mr Tubby, because Goosey Gander could hear him snoring in the cottage. It wasn't Farmer Giles, because he was big and fat, and this figure was lean and small.

It was the poacher, Jim Hookey! The farmer had driven him away the week before, and told him he would put him in prison if he caught any more hares on his land, and Jim had said he would pay back the farmer somehow. Now he was going to open the field gate and drive out the lambs and the sheep so that they would all be scattered about and lost by the next morning.

Goosey Gander gave a loud hiss of rage. He was very fond of his master and he didn't like to think of how angry the farmer might be with Mr Tubby if he found all his sheep and lambs strayed from the field. He would think that Mr Tubby had forgotten to shut the gate.

'*Ss-ss-ss-ss-ss-ss-ss-ss!*' hissed Goosey Gander and waddled out of the shed. He walked to the field gate and looked about for the poacher. He was driving the sheep and lambs towards the open gate. Goosey Gander chuckled to himself and hid in the hedge. Just as the sheep and lambs came running up, he flew out with great wings flapping, and cackled at the top of his voice. 'Cackle, cackle, cackle, cackle, cackle, cackle!'

The sheep stopped in fright, and ran right away up the field again. The poacher stopped in fright too, and the gander flew right at him and flapped his strong wings in his face.

'Ooooh!' cried the poacher, terrified, and he ran helter-skelter out of the gate and rushed down the lane as fast as his legs could carry him. He thought the gander was an old witch.

Goosey Gander watched him go. He was very pleased. He saw that all the sheep were safely at the other end of the field, and then he waddled to the gate. He shut it carefully and then put the catch in place with his beak.

He turned to go back to his shed, when he saw a big fat man watching him. It was Farmer Giles. Goosey Gander liked him, so he said, 'Cackle! cackle!' very softly and rubbed his head against him.

'Well, Goosey Gander, I saw all you did!' said Farmer Giles. 'You're the cleverest bird I've ever seen! I saw you turn back the sheep, frighten the poacher and shut the gate. Well, you've saved me a lot of trouble and loss, and I'll tell your master in the morning what a fine bird you are!'

Goosey Gander waddled back home to his shed and went to sleep. In the morning he went to knock on the door to waken Mr Tubby, as he always did.

Farmer Giles came down to see Mr Tubby after breakfast, and was just in time to catch Mrs Tubby going off to market with Goosey Gander. She had meant to sell him that very day.

'Where are you taking that goose to?' asked Farmer Giles.

'To sell him at the market, to pay our doctor's bill,' answered Mrs Tubby. 'Poor bird, we're very fond of him, but he's the only thing we've got to sell.'

'Well, let me tell you what I saw him doing last night,' said the farmer, and he told Mrs Tubby all he had seen. She was most astonished, and called Mr Tubby from the sheep field to tell him all about it.

'You mustn't sell a clever gander like that,' said the farmer. 'I'll pay your doctor's bill for you, and you shall keep him. He saved my sheep for me, and I'd like to do something for him in return. I'm sure he'd like to stay with you instead of being sold.'

Goosey Gander was overjoyed! He flew at the farmer in delight and almost knocked him over.

'Cackle, cackle, cackle!' he cried. 'Cackle, cackle, cackle!'

He still lives with Mr and Mrs Tubby, and is very happy. Every Christmas, Farmer Giles sends him a present, and what do you think it is? A big tin of peas! He simply loves to eat them, and all the time he hisses happily – like this: '*Ss-ss-ss-ss-ss-ss-ss!*'

Snapdragon Snippets

Snapdragon Snippets

THE SNIPPET pixies lived in the mushroom fields, where houses were cheap. As soon as a fine mushroom grew up, the Snippets snipped out a door and a window, made a stairway inside the stalk and a room inside the mushroom top, and hey presto! There was a house big enough for two Snippets at least!

But one day it happened that a boy came along who saw the mushrooms and picked them – and, dear me, what a surprise for him when he saw the doors and windows! The Snippets flew out at once and fled away from the field. The boy followed in glee. He thought they were butterflies or moths, and as he carried a net with him he meant to catch them.

The Snippets flew on and on, panting hard. They flew over a cornfield and the boy rushed after them. They flew down the lane, they flew through a wood, and at last, quite tired out, they flew into a garden.

'We can't fly any further!' panted one little Snippet, sinking down to the ground like a tiny bubble. 'That boy will have to catch us!'

'What's the matter?' asked a bumblebee nearby.

The Snippets told him. 'There's a boy, look, coming in at the gate now!' they groaned. 'Whatever can we do? There doesn't seem anywhere to hide, bumblebee.'

'Quick! I'll show you a place!' buzzed the velvety bee. 'Follow me!'

He flew to a red snapdragon. He alighted on the lower part and pressed it down so that the snapdragon opened its 'bunny-mouth'. In went the bee – and the mouth of the snapdragon closed behind him so that not even a leg could be seen! He pushed himself out backwards to the surprised Snippets.

'There you are! Get inside any of these snapdragon flowers and you'll be well hidden!'

The Snippets gave little high squeals of glee. Each one flew up to a red, pink or yellow snapdragon, and pressed hard on the lower lip of the flower. The mouth opened – the Snippets slipped in – the mouth closed up! Not a wing was to be seen, not even a tiny bare foot!

The boy banged the garden gate and looked round. 'Where are those strange little butterflies?' he said, holding his net ready to catch them. 'I know they flew into this garden, for I saw them. Where have they hidden themselves?'

He went to the flowerbed. He set the flowers swinging to and fro, so that he might frighten any butterfly into the air. But the Snippets were safe, though their hiding places swung about as the boy pushed them with his net. It was like being in a cosy hammock. The flowers smelt lovely, too – they made a wonderful hiding place!

The boy soon left the garden, and it was safe for the

Snippets to come out. They peeped from their strange hiding place and nodded to one another. 'We can't go back to our mushroom houses now,' they cried. 'Shall we live here instead?'

Everybody thought it was a good idea. They went to buy soft yellow blankets for beds from the gnome under the hedge, and that was all they needed. Each night they crept into the bunny-mouths of the snapdragons and slept on their hammocks of yellow down, and they probably do still.

You won't find them there in the daytime, for then they are at work snipping up fallen flower petals to make frocks and coats – but you might press open a snapdragon gently and see if you can find the Snippets' downy yellow beds made ready for the night!

Ladybird, Ladybird,
Fly Away Home

Ladybird, Ladybird, Fly Away Home

ONCE WHEN Alistair was walking round his garden, he saw a big spider's web. He stopped to look at it – and as he watched, a little red ladybird with pretty black spots on her back flew straight into the web!

The web trembled – and out from under a nearby leaf rushed a big spider, hungry for a meal.

The ladybird struggled hard, but the web was sticky, and she could not free her feet or her wings. Alistair was sorry for her.

He picked up a tiny stick and began to cut the web round the ladybird. The spider was frightened and went back to her hiding place, angry that her web was being spoilt.

'I'm sorry to spoil your beautiful web, spider, but I rather like ladybirds,' said Alistair, and he took the tiny insect on to the end of his stick. The ladybird ran down the stick and on to his finger.

She began to clean the web from her body. Alistair thought she was a dear little beetle. He watched her tuck her wings under her red wing cases, and then clean her legs thoroughly.

'I like you,' he said. 'I've done you a good turn, though I don't expect you know it. Hello, Mum – look what I've just rescued from the spider – a little red ladybird with black spots on her back!'

'Nice little thing!' said Mother. 'Well, you've done her a good turn. Maybe she will do us one some day!'

Alistair laughed. 'Oh, she can't, Mum. We're so big and she's so little. Ladybird, ladybird, fly away home!'

The ladybird flew away – but she didn't fly far. She flew to Alistair's small garden. He had a rose tree there that he was very fond of – but oh dear, it was covered with greenfly, and they were sucking the juice from the little new buds and leaves too.

The ladybird laid her eggs there. Then she flew off again. The eggs hatched out in a day or two. From them came funny little black beetles. They rushed about, up and down the rose tree, very lively indeed.

Alistair saw them one day. 'Mother, what are these little black beetles?' he said. 'Do you see them on my rose tree? Oh dear, what with greenfly and the black beetles my poor tree will soon be dead. I keep picking off these greenfly but they come again the next day. Shall I pick off the new little beetles?'

'Oh no, Alistair!' said his mother. 'Of course not. They are the children of the ladybird! She laid her eggs on your tree because she knew that there was greenfly food for them. Watch how they attack and eat the green blight!'

Sure enough, the little black beetles did eat the greenfly! They cleared stem after stem, leaf after leaf, and soon the tree was completely clear again. Alistair was glad.

'I suppose these beetles will one day turn into ladybirds themselves,' he said. 'Oh Mother, I'm glad I rescued the ladybird! I did her a good turn – and now she has done me one too. I shall always put ladybirds on my rose trees when I find them, now!'

You can too, if you like. They will certainly be very good little friends to you!

Jimmy's Robin

Jimmy's Robin

IN JIMMY'S garden lived a fine cock robin. You should have seen him! He had a beautiful red breast and the brightest black eyes, and he flew down beside Jimmy every time the little boy went to dig in his garden.

Jimmy gave the robin crumbs each day, and he often sang a little sweet song to Jimmy, and once, for just a moment, he flew on to Jimmy's head and stood there! Wasn't that friendly!

Then one day Jimmy was ill. He had to go to bed, and the little robin missed him badly. He hunted all over the garden for Jimmy, but he was nowhere to be seen. So the robin thought he would go and look in the house. Perhaps Jimmy was there!

He looked in all the windows – and at last he found Jimmy, lying in bed, looking very miserable, for the little boy was lonely. The robin flew in at the open window and then sat on the bottom of Jimmy's bed.

'Tweet, tweet, chirry, chirry, chee!' he sang. Jimmy opened his eyes and sat up in delight.

'Why, it's my robin!' he said. 'Oh, robin, how nice of you to come and find me! It's been so dull lying here in bed! Do come and see me every day!'

'Tweet, tweet, I will!' said the robin.. He flew down on to Jimmy's blanket and sang a little song there and then he flew out of the window again. He had thought of such a good idea! He had a little wife and they were looking for a good place to build their nest. What fun it would be if they could find a place in Jimmy's bedroom! Jimmy was such a nice boy, and the little robin would like to build somewhere near his friend.

He found his wife and told her his good idea. Then together they flew back to Jimmy's bedroom and looked into every nook and corner to see if they could find a good place to put their nest.

'What about behind this bookcase by Jimmy's bed?' said the robin. 'There is just room.'

'Tweet, chirry chee!' said the wife. 'Yes, that will be fine!'

So, for the next few days, Jimmy had a lovely time, watching the little robins build their nest in his bedroom! He didn't tell anyone, because he was afraid that his mother might say they were making a mess. He just lay and watched the little birds fly in and out – sometimes with a wisp of root, sometimes with two or three dead leaves, sometimes with a bit of moss.

One day the robin pecked a few hairs out of Jimmy's hairbrush! Jimmy did laugh! The hair went into the nest too. Then the robin's wife sat down on her cosy nest behind the bookcase and laid four pretty, red-spotted eggs. Jimmy could just see them if he peeped behind the bookcase. It really was very exciting!

'I can't understand how it is that Jimmy is so good and happy, staying all this time in bed!' said his mother to the doctor. 'He is just as good as gold!'

Jimmy knew why he was so happy and good. It was because he had two friends living behind his bookcase. But he wasn't going to say a word!

One day the eggs hatched out into tiny baby birds. The two robins sang loudly for joy. Jimmy sang for joy too! He was just as pleased as the robins. He peeped behind the bookcase and looked at the baby birds each day. Sometimes the two robins would fly off to get food for them, and Jimmy would look after them. He promised the robin that he would not let Pussy come into the room.

And then the little robins grew so big that it was time for them to fly away. And do you know, they all got out of the nest and flew about the room! Just imagine that! Jimmy laughed so loudly – and just at that moment his door opened and in came Mother with the doctor!

'Well!' said Mother, in surprise. 'Wherever did all these birds come from?'

And then Jimmy had to tell his mother about the

nest and show her and the doctor where it was built behind the bookcase. Mother was so surprised!

'But I am very sad now,' said Jimmy, 'because, you see, the babies are flying away and I won't see the robins anymore. They will be about the garden, with their father and mother. It is time they flew out of this room.'

'And it is time you flew out of this room too!' said the doctor, smiling. 'It is lovely sunny weather and you are to lie out in the garden all day long now – so you will be able to see your robins all the time!'

Jimmy was so pleased – and now he and the robins are in the garden together, and Jimmy is nearly well again. He has six tame robins – isn't he lucky?

The Witch's Egg

The Witch's Egg

ONCE UPON a time Sneaky the elf peeped into Witch Upadee's kitchen and saw her working a spell. First she took a small chocolate Easter egg and put it on a plate. Sneaky knew the kind. You could buy them for a ha'pence each, and they were filled with sticky cream inside. He sat himself on the windowsill and watched to see what happened next.

Witch Upadee took a peacock's feather and stroked the tiny egg. Then she blew on it hard and chanted, 'Grow, grow. Quick and slow. Make yourself sweet for witches to eat. Grow, grow. Quick and slow!'

And, to Sneaky's enormous astonishment, that tiny

chocolate egg began to grow big on the plate! How it grew! How it swelled up! My goodness, Sneaky did feel hungry when he saw that great egg of chocolate, all ready to be eaten, growing bigger and bigger! He nearly fell off the windowsill in surprise – and then, what a shock he got! Witch Upadee saw him and gave a shout of rage. She picked up her broom and swept him right off her windowsill!

'You nasty little sneaking thing, always peeping and prying! Go away! You *shan't* see my spells!'

But Sneaky had seen enough. He ran home grinning and rubbing his hands. *He* would make a chocolate egg grow like that, too – and my, what a lot of money he would make by selling it!

He bought a chocolate egg and took it home. He set it on a plate and then went to borrow a peacock's feather from his friend next door. He stroked the little egg with it, and then blew on it hard, feeling tremendously excited. Then he chanted loudly the magic song, 'Grow, grow. Quick and slow. Make yourself sweet for *fairies* to eat. Grow,

grow. Quick and slow!'

The chocolate egg began to grow. How it grew! You really should have seen it. It was a most marvellous sight. First it was as big as a hen's egg. Then as big as a goose's. Then as big as a swan's. Then as large as an ostrich's. Then as big as a coal scuttle – and it went on growing. Sneaky was delighted. He danced round in joy, watching the egg grow.

It grew and it grew. Crack! It broke the plate with its weight. But Sneaky didn't mind. He could buy lots of new plates with the money for that lovely egg! That the egg grew bigger than the table – and crack! One of the legs gave way, and down went the table and the egg, too. But still it went on growing!

When it was as big as a large wheelbarrow Sneaky thought it was big enough. After all, he had to get it out of the door and take it to market – it wouldn't do for it to get *too* big! So he shouted to it. 'Stop! Don't grow any more, egg!' But the egg didn't take a bit of notice, no, not a bit. It just went on growing – and however much Sneaky begged it to stop it simply wouldn't. Sneaky didn't know the right words to say, you see! Well, it grew – and it grew – and it grew – and at last it couldn't grow any more, because it was as big as the room itself – and poor Sneaky was squashed flat in one corner. And then in pressing itself against the ceiling, the egg broke! Out came a great stream of sticky cream – all over poor Sneaky! After that the egg stopped growing, for the spell was broken.

But do you know – the only way Sneaky could get out of the room was by eating his way through the egg! It took him two days – and oh, the mess he was in! And now, if you meet a small elf who says he simply can't *bear* Easter eggs, just ask him his name. It's sure to be Sneaky!

The Wrong
Dinnertime

The Wrong Dinnertime

'MUMMY, MAY we go and play in the fields at the bottom of the garden today?' asked Ann. 'It's such a lovely day, and we won't sit down on the damp grass. The little lambs are in the field, and it's fun to watch them.'

'Very well,' said her mother, 'but you must come when I call you. I shall come to the kitchen door and call "Cuckoo!" loudly – and you must cuckoo back and come straight in to dinner.'

'Yes, we promise to do that,' said Gerry. 'We won't be a minute late!'

Off they went. Gerry took his box of toy soldiers,

and Ann took her favourite doll.

'I can put my toy soldiers out on the top of one of the henhouses in the field,' said Gerry. 'They will look fine, all shining in the sun.'

'And I shall take my doll for a walk all round the field and back,' said Ann. 'I might find one or two primroses by the stream. If I do, Dolly can wear them in her hair.'

Gerry put out all his soldiers one by one and marched them up the henhouse. They did look grand. Ann took her doll round the field and found four primroses. She was so pleased. She put two in her own hair and two in Dolly's.

'Come and see my soldiers, Ann!' shouted Gerry. 'They are all in a long line!'

Ann ran over to look at them – and just then a sound came to their ears.

'Cuckoo!'

'Goodness! It's dinnertime already!' said Ann, in dismay. 'And we've hardly been here any time. Hurry up and put your soldiers away, Gerry. You know what

Mummy said – we were to come at once.'

'All right,' said Gerry, and he scooped all his soldiers into the box. He put the lid on and the two children trotted back home. They went indoors and found their mother washing some cups at the sink.

'What are you back here for?' she asked in surprise. 'I thought you went to play in the field.'

'Well, you called us in,' said Ann. 'We came at once.'

'Bless us, child, I didn't call you!' said her mother. 'It's only twelve o'clock. You've another hour till dinnertime.'

'But, Mum, we heard you call us,' said Gerry.

'Well, you heard wrong then,' said their mother, wiping the cups dry. 'Go along, now. I expect it was someone else you heard.'

Ann and Gerry ran off again. This time Gerry took his wooden train and Ann took her ball. Soon they were back in the field with the lambs again, and Ann was throwing her ball up and catching it. The lambs came round to watch, and when she missed the ball, so that it went bouncing towards them on the grass, they skipped off on their funny little legs, pretending to be quite frightened.

Gerry filled his wooden engine with stones and pretended that he was taking goods from place to place. Just as he was filling it for the third time, he stood up and listened.

'Ann!' he cried. 'Time to go home, I heard Mum calling.'

'You didn't!' said Ann.

'I did!' said Gerry.

'Didn't!' said Ann.

'Well, listen then, and see,' said Gerry. So they listened – and sure enough, Ann heard 'Cuckoo!'

'Sorry, Gerry,' she said. 'You're right. It is Mummy – but I didn't think it could possibly be one o'clock.'

Back home they went at top speed – and this time their mother was hanging out some clothes in the garden.

'Back again!' she said in astonishment. 'What's brought you home again so soon?'

'But you called us again!' said Ann, in the greatest

surprise. 'You did really. We both heard you.'

'Darling, I didn't call you,' said their mother. 'It's not quite half past twelve.'

'Well, who could it be, then, calling us like that?' said Gerry, puzzled.

'Let's go back to the fields and see if we can see anyone hiding,' said Ann. 'Oh, Gerry – it might be a fairy! Just playing us a trick, you know!'

They ran back to the field and hunted carefully all round the hedge. Then they heard the voice again, 'Cuckoo!'

'There *is* some one hiding near by,' said Ann. 'I heard that call again – and I'm sure it's not Mummy this time. Oh, do let's find whoever it is, Gerry.'

But although they hunted everywhere, not a boy or a girl or a pixie could they see. Not one. It was most disappointing.

'Cuckoo! Cuckoo!' The children heard a voice in the distance and saw their mother waving to them.

'It is Mummy this time!' said Ann. 'Come on, Gerry.'

They ran home for the third time – and it was their

mother calling them. As they washed their hands they told her how puzzled they were. As they were telling her, a voice called clearly, not far off, 'Cuckoo!'

'Did you hear that?' said Ann excitedly. 'Do you suppose it's a fairy having a joke?'

Their mother laughed till the tears ran down her face. 'My dears,' she said, 'what silly-billies you are! That's the cuckoo, come back again for the summer! He's been calling all morning! Did you really think it was me who was calling so often?'

'The cuckoo!' cried the children in delight, and rushed to the door at once. Sure enough, it was – they heard his clear call coming down the hillside, 'Cuckoo! Cuckoo!'

'Cuckoo!' the children shouted back. 'You tricked us this morning, cuckoo, and made us go home twice for nothing, but we're very glad you're back again!'

'Cuckoo!' shouted the cuckoo – and they heard him all the time they were having dinner. He was just as glad to be back as they were glad to have him!

Second Walk in April

Second Walk in April

Birds in April

ONE MORNING Uncle Merry saw three excited children rushing through his garden gate. He leant out of his window and waved.

'Uncle Merry! We've heard the cuckoo! We've heard the cuckoo! We've heard the cuckoo!' called Pat, in excitement.

'We've all heard him at the same time,' said John. 'Oh, it was lovely to hear him again!'

'I heard him too,' shouted down Uncle Merry. A loud barking from below the window inside the room told the children that Fergus had evidently heard the cuckoo as well!

'It's Saturday. Are you going to take us for a walk?' asked Janet. 'This morning or this afternoon?'

Uncle Merry looked up at the cloud-swept April-blue sky. 'This morning,' he said, 'I meant to do some work – but how can I sit indoors on a day when three excited children come and tell me that the cuckoo is back? I feel I want a day off. Ten minutes – and I'll be with you!'

So, with Fergus the Scottie scampering madly round on his short legs, his tail wagging so fast that it could hardly be seen, the five soon set off down the familiar lanes, now green with hawthorn hedges on each side, the dainty stitchwort embroidering the banks, and the golden celandines turning polished stars to the sun. John couldn't walk. He skipped, he ran, he trotted, he capered. He said it was too happy a day for walking.

'There's the cuckoo again!' said Pat, as the lovely double note sounded on the wind. 'Oh, it does seem like summertime to hear that! I love the cuckoo, don't you, Uncle Merry?'

'Well, no, I can't say I do,' said Uncle Merry. 'He's not really a favourite of mine, except that I, like you, like to hear his call in the springtime. But, you see, the cuckoo leads a lazy life – he leaves all the work of building a nest and of bringing up and feeding young ones, to *other* birds.'

'Doesn't he make a nest then?' said John, in surprise. 'I thought all birds built nests.'

'Not the cuckoo,' said Uncle Merry. 'The hen cuckoo puts her egg in another bird's nest, first taking out an egg from the nest to make room for it. The bird who owns the nest doesn't seem to notice that it is a strange egg, and when it hatches into a bare, black, ugly nestling, the bird cares for it and brings it up as if it were her own.'

'How queer!' said Pat. 'It doesn't seem to be fair, does it?'

'No,' said Uncle Merry. 'The funny thing is that when the cuckoo nestling grows, it becomes much bigger than its little stepmother, and she has to sit on the baby cuckoo's shoulder to feed it!'

'Cuckoo! Cuckoo!' called a voice, and over their heads flew a big grey bird, with a barred chest. 'There goes the cuckoo!' said Uncle Merry. 'Probably she has only just returned to this country. She has spent the winter far away in warmer lands, feeding on the insects there.'

'What other birds will be back soon?' asked John. 'I know the swallows go away, don't they?'

'Yes – and the martins and swifts, the nightingales, the whitethroats, the chiff-chaffs, and others,' said Uncle Merry. 'Listen – I do believe I can hear the chiffchaff now!'

They all stood still and listened. They had come to a little copse of trees in which many birds were singing. 'What's his song like?' whispered John.

'Oh, he says his name over and over again,' said Uncle Merry. 'There it is – listen – chiff, chaff, chiff, chaff, chiff, chaff!'

They all heard it in delight. 'Now I will always know the chiffchaff's voice,' said John, pleased.

They left the trees and went on, Fergus putting his head down every hole they came to. Suddenly Uncle Merry stopped and looked upwards, intense pleasure on his face. The children looked up too. They saw a steel-blue, long-tailed bird sweeping through the air, and a few more on the telegraph wires, making a musical twittering sound. *Feet-a-feetit, feet-a-feetit!* they said.

'The swallows!' said Uncle Merry. 'Bless them, they're back again! How I love them!'

The children loved them too, as they watched them flying swiftly through the air, forked tails streaming behind them. With them flew birds rather like them, but with a good deal of white about them, both underneath and on the back. Their tails were not so long.

'Are those shorter-tailed birds swallows too?' asked John.

'They belong to the swallow family,' said Uncle Merry. 'They are house martins. They build their nests of mud, under the eaves of houses. You must have seen them. The swallows put their nests on rafters or beams in barns and sheds, and that is why we call them barn swallows. The martin up there is called the house martin because he likes to build near our houses. There is another little martin too, brown and white, the sand martin. He builds his nest in a hole in a bank or quarry, together with many of his friends.'

'I shall never know them all,' sighed Janet, looking at the swallows and martins. 'Isn't there another bird like the swallows, Uncle – the swift?'

'Ah yes,' said Uncle Merry, 'but he doesn't come until a bit later. He isn't a swallow. He is rather like them to look at simply because he leads the same aerial life, and therefore needs the same kind of wings and long tail. He is sooty-black, not blue. I'll point him out to you when he arrives.'

'There is such a lot to learn,' said Janet. 'I don't know how you remember everything, Uncle.'

'Only because I love the countryside, and am always looking around and noticing things; and then, of course, because I love them I read about them in my books,' said Uncle Merry. 'You can do the same – and perhaps when you are my age you will know ten times more than I do!'

Janet thought that was quite impossible. She slipped her hand into Uncle Merry's and thought how lovely it would be to know so much and love so much. She was already beginning to understand the deep delight and intense joy he showed and felt in the host of things that made up the countryside. It was something only those could know who felt it themselves too – and Janet was beginning to feel it. She felt it when she looked at the sheet of golden celandines; she felt it when she saw a tangle of white stitchworts, starry against the green bank. She squeezed her uncle's hand.

'When I see things like that, I feel sometimes as if I'd like to write a poem about them, and keep them for ever!' she half-whispered.

Uncle Merry looked down at her, a wise smile in his brown eyes. 'You feel as artists do when they long to paint something,' he said. 'They want to catch the beautiful thing their eyes see and keep it prisoner for ever on their canvas. Poets want to capture it and hold it imprisoned in words. Musicians entangle it in music. Janet, it is a precious gift to be able to feel like that. Let it grow!'

Well, I may be silly sometimes, thought Janet to herself, *but Uncle Merry wouldn't talk to me like that if I was really and truly stupid!*

The birds were singing madly that morning, though many of them were busy with nest-making. The children saw them carrying leaves and bits of moss in their beaks. They heard the many songs – and they heard a new one, most delicious and sweet.

'The blackcap!' said Uncle Merry, listening. 'What rich clear notes it has! Almost as fine as the blackbird – so mellow and full. How lucky we are in this country to have so many singing birds!'

'Uncle Merry, what is that little bird over there – like a sparrow?' asked Pat, pointing to a small bird looking for insects in the ditch.

'It's not like a sparrow,' said John at once, 'except

that it's brown! Look at its thin beak, Pat – sparrows have a big clumsy beak. That bird looks more like a robin.'

'John, I sometimes think you are the sharpest of all you three children,' said Uncle Merry. 'You really do notice things. That bird is a hedge sparrow – but, as you say, it isn't really a sparrow. You have only to see its beak to know that it is an insect-eater, not a seed-eater like the real sparrow.

They all watched the sober-brown bird. It made some funny little movements with its wings.

'It shuffles them!' said John.

'Its other name is shufflewing,' said Uncle Merry. 'You can see why!'

'Uncle – it's flown up into that hedge there,' said Pat, as the bird flew into a green hawthorn nearby. 'Has it got its nest there, do you think?'

The bird flew out again. Uncle Merry went quietly to the hedge and parted a few twigs. He saw a nest there, with a sitting bird. The bird flew off in fright. Uncle Merry beckoned the children.

'I hate frightening a sitting bird,' he said, 'but you must really see one of the prettiest sights in the bird kingdom. Look!'

The children looked – and there in the nest were four hedge sparrow eggs as blue as the sky above – the purest, brightest blue imaginable, gleaming against the brown of the nest-cup.

'Oh, lovely!' said Janet, her eyes starry with delight. 'Quite, quite perfect!'

They left the nest of eggs for the mother to come back to, and went on their way. A big bumblebee sailed past and Janet nearly squealed, but not quite. Fergus jumped up at it in indignation, for it went very near his nose.

'*Zooooom!*' said the bee, and sailed away.

'He spent the winter sleeping in a hole in a bank,' said Uncle Merry. 'Lovely thing, isn't he, with his velvet coat of thick fur?'

'Uncle Merry, we haven't found a single new flower,' said Pat. 'Isn't that queer?'

'Not very,' said Uncle Merry with a laugh. 'We've

been looking up into the sky most of the time, haven't we, and seeing the birds? We can't look down at the ground as well. But now we will. Come along – who will see a new flower first?'

John did, of course. His eyes never seemed to miss anything. Janet was a bit of a dreamer, and sometimes seemed to look at things without seeing them. Pat was full of eagerness and saw plenty of things, but because he didn't look at them carefully, like John, he made a good many mistakes.

'Here's a pretty little flower!' cried John, and he picked a stem from the bank. The flowers were small and rosy-purple, and each of the petals was notched in the centre of its broadest edge. The leaves were almost round, and downy with hairs, deeply cut at the edges.

'It's the dove's foot cranesbill,' said Uncle Merry, 'one of our many pretty little wild geraniums.'

'Why is it called cranesbill?' asked John. 'I can't see anything like a crane's beak in the flower.'

'No – you must wait for the seeds to form before

you see that,' said Uncle Merry. 'Then you will see a long beak growing out from the middle of the flower, just like a crane's long bill.'

'Is this another dove's foot cranesbill?' asked Pat, picking another flower.

John gave it a glance. 'Of course it isn't!' he said. 'The flower may be purple-pink, but look at the leaves, silly! They are quite different!'

So they were, all cut up into fingers, not a bit rounded as were the soft leaves of the dove's foot. 'I've seen these leaves in the autumn – they go a bright red, don't they?' said John, remembering.

'Quite right,' said Uncle Merry. 'This flower, that Pat has found, is the herb Robert, another wild geranium. Look at the two closely and see the differences – you especially, Pat. See how the petals of the dove's foot are notched, and its leaves rounded – and notice the larger flowers of the herb Robert, and its cut-up leaves. Later on, when these plants go to seed, we will see how they each grow beak-like seed vessels.'

The children found more flowers after that – one that Pat called a yellow dead-nettle, because it looked rather like it.

'It is the yellow archangel,' said Uncle Merry, 'and it belongs to the lip family of course. You can see its resemblance to the other members we know, though its leaves are not so nettle-like as those of the white dead-nettle. See the lower lip – a platform for the bee to alight on – and look into the upper lip, where you will find the stamens and pistil. They are carefully placed there, so that when the bee seeks for nectar his back will brush against the pollen and he will fly off covered with it, to rub it against the pistil of the next archangel flower he visits.'

'I really do think the flowers are clever, the way they work with the insects to get their pollen sent about,' said Janet. 'It's wonderful! They haven't got brains to think, as we have, and yet all these ideas are there, worked out to perfection. It's mysterious.'

'It is – most mysterious,' said Uncle Merry. 'Look – there's the first cowslip! I really must mention it, because I feel *I* would like to claim a new flower, too, this morning!'

The cowslip nodded its head in the wind as it grew in the grass nearby.

'I know it belongs to the primrose family,' said Janet, picking it. 'Oh – it does smell sweet! There will be thousands of these out here next month, Uncle. We must gather a big bunch then to take home to Mother.'

The ramblers had walked in a big circle, and were now almost home. Fergus scampered ahead, and stopped at the usual rabbit hole. His head disappeared, and a shower of earth came up from behind him.

Pat went to pull him out, for once Fergus really got going, nothing would make him come along home. As he bent down to get hold of the dog, he saw some big leaves growing nearby. He stared at them. He tried to remember something. *Big cobwebby leaves – the shape of a young horse's foot – coltsfoot leaves!* thought Pat, using his brain well. He gave a shout. 'Look! Coltsfoot leaves! I've found *those* first, anyway!'

'Bright boy!' said Uncle Merry, looking really pleased. 'Yes – they are. Do you remember the coltsfoot flowers growing here earlier? See – there are some seeding now. Aren't the leaves big, and do you see how cobwebby they seem to be? I am glad you found them, Pat. I had forgotten all about them.'

Pat felt really proud. Now *he* had had a word of praise from Uncle Merry too. They all went home in a very good temper, and just got in before a large rainstorm swept over the countryside, drenching everything in a few minutes.

'Our next walk is in May,' said Uncle Merry. 'We shall wish we had a hundred eyes then, there will be so much to see!'

The Buttercup Spell

The Buttercup Spell

DO YOU know the story of the buttercup spell? Well, let me tell it to you.

It happened that a farmer many, many years ago, had a wonderful cow called Buttercup. Buttercup gave beautiful, creamy milk and from it the farmer's wife made the finest golden butter in all the kingdom. Even the king and queen sent a servant each day to buy some of the delicious butter for them to eat with their bread.

And then one day the farmer's wife found that there was a thief who was creeping into her dairy each night and stealing some of the big golden pot of butter! But no one had seen the thief. Who on earth could it be?

'Is it Diana, the dairymaid?' she wondered. 'No, she's an honest girl. Is it Dan the cowman? No, he has a cow of his own and so he can have butter whenever he likes. Is it Johnnie who looks after the horses? No, he never even comes near the dairy. It can't be Jill the goose-girl either, because everyone knows she never eats butter!'

But still, night by night, the butter kept disappearing and yet no dog ever barked when the thief came.

'It must be someone the dogs know!' said the farmer. 'We'll keep watch.'

But though they kept watch every night, still the butter went. No one came in at the door. No one crept in at a window. Then who took the butter?

The farmer's wife went to her great-grandmother, who was a witch, and told her the whole story. The old dame listened and nodded her head.

'Ah – it must certainly be someone that loves

butter and craves for it!' she said. 'Someone who is very clever – clever enough to take it each night under your very noses! Now which cow did you say gives the finest butter?'

'Buttercup,' said the farmer's wife. 'And she's well named, for her creamy milk makes the butter that is sent up to the royal palace every day!'

'Ah, Buttercup!' said the old dame. 'Well, then, you must go out to the field and pick me the finest buttercup there that you can see. Bring it back to me and I will walk to your farm with you, and then I will soon be able to find the thief who keeps stealing your butter!'

The farmer's wife picked a fine golden buttercup, whose cup shone just as if it had been freshly polished. The old witch walked back to the farm with her, and when they got there she spoke to the farmer.

'Call all your workers here, every one of them!'

One by one they came and stood round the old dame in surprise.

'Don't be afraid,' she said. 'I'm only using a simple

buttercup spell that never did anyone any harm! Step forward, Diana the dairymaid.'

Diana stood in front of the old dame, half afraid. She knew the old woman was a witch. What kind of spell was she using? A buttercup spell? She had certainly never heard of a spell like that before.

The old woman took the buttercup and held it under the dairymaid's chin for a moment. Then she shook her head and pushed the girl away.

'She's not the one we want,' she said. 'Come forward, Johnnie, the horseman.' Johnnie stepped forward, feeling very puzzled.

The old woman held the buttercup under his chin, peering there as she did so. She shook her head again. 'He's not the one,' she said.

One by one all the farm workers came up to the old dame and held up their chins for her to hold the buttercup there. But each time she shook her head.

'It's none of these,' she said. 'Is this all? Are there no more workers on your farm?'

'Well, there's only Jill the goose-girl,' said the

farmer's wife. 'And she's out on the common with her geese. She never eats butter, so she can't be the thief.'

'Fetch her,' commanded the old woman. 'I must try every single one who works here with the spell.'

The other workers went back to their tasks and the goose-girl was sent for. She came with her geese behind her, a ragged little thing with big, frightened eyes.

'Here, lass, come and stand by me,' commanded the old woman. 'Do you like butter?'

'Yes, I like it very much. But I never eat it,' said the goose-girl in a scared voice. 'I give my share to my mother. She's been ill for a long time.'

'Stand still while I hold this buttercup under your chin,' said the old woman, and the goose-girl lifted her chin and stood there, trembling.

The old dame held the buttercup under the girl's chin – and everyone saw a bright golden glow there, that shone like a small sun.

'Here is the thief,' said the old woman. 'Jill the goose-girl, who says she never eats butter. She must be punished, for she is certainly wicked.'

'I'm not, I'm not,' wept the girl. 'As I said, I do like butter very much, but I tell my mother that I don't, so that she may have my share. But she has been so ill lately that I had to steal a big pat of it for her each night. She needs butter and milk and eggs so badly, mistress, to help her get stronger!'

'But however did you steal it?' asked the farmer's wife, who was feeling terribly sorry for the trembling girl.

'Mistress, I crept up on to the roof every night, and let down a basket through the skylight,' wept the poor goose-girl. 'I put a long stick down and knocked a pat of butter into the basket and then drew it up again. The dogs didn't bark because, you see, they knew me.'

'Poor child,' said the farmer's wife kindly. 'You did wrong, but I see how much you love your mother. Promise never to steal again and your mother shall have all the butter and milk and eggs that she needs.'

'My buttercup spell found her out!' said the old witch. 'And it will always find out those people who love butter and long to have it! That spell will last for a thousand years!'

She was right, wasn't she? Hold a buttercup under anyone's chin and see the spell still at work – anyone who loves butter will at once show a bright golden glow there, like a little sun, shining and gleaming! Have you ever tried it? What a strange bit of old, old magic!

Salt on a Bird's Tail

Salt on a Bird's Tail

HAVE YOU ever heard that you can catch a bird if you put salt on its tail? I expect you have – and maybe you have tried to do it too.

There was once a little girl called Alice who loved birds very much. She fed them all through the winter, and she gave them water to drink and a bowl to bath in during the summer.

They grew very tame indeed and the robin would perch on the handle of her garden spade whenever she left it sticking into the earth. But not one of the birds would let Alice hold it in her hand so that she might feel the warm body and fluffy feathers.

'I do so wish the birds loved me enough to trust me to pick them up gently,' Alice said to her Uncle Jim, who was also very fond of birds. 'I've never held a bird in my hand, Uncle – and they do look as if they would be so lovely to hold for a moment or two. I'd like to feel them against my neck, all soft and warm.'

'Well,' said Uncle Jim with a laugh, 'don't you know how to catch a bird, Alice? Just put salt on its tail, and you've got it!'

'Oh, really, Uncle Jim?' said Alice, in delight. 'I'll try then.'

So the very next day Alice went to the sideboard and took the little glass salt cellar out. She emptied some of the salt into a paper sweet bag and then put the salt cellar back. Out she went into the garden.

Now, where are there any birds? thought the little girl. *Oh – there's a sparrow on the lawn!*

She crept up to it, nearer and nearer – but the bird saw her and flew off with a chirrup of fright. Alice waited till another bird appeared.

'There's the pretty chaffinch on the grass,' she said.

'I'd love to catch him and hold him gently.' So she crept softly over the grass to where the chaffinch was pecking around.

She put her finger and thumb into the bag of salt – but the chaffinch heard the little rustle of the paper and flew off with a whirr of his pretty wings.

Alice was very disappointed. She wondered if perhaps she ought to hide in the bushes – then the birds wouldn't see her. So she squeezed herself into a bush and waited patiently. A blackbird came and perched just above her head. He flicked his tail up and down. Alice quietly got ready a pinch of salt – but he suddenly saw her, gave his loud alarm cry, and flew off.

'Bother!' said Alice. 'It's too bad. The birds see me and get a fright. Really it's silly of them, because they know I'm their friend!'

Then she thought it would be a good idea if she fetched some breadcrumbs and threw them down. The birds would come to get them and she could perhaps quickly throw a pinch of salt on their tails as they pecked about.

So she fetched some stale pieces of bread and broke them up into crumbs. Soon the lawn was white with crumbs and the birds called to one another to come and feed.

Down flew three sparrows. Down flew the robin. The blackbird came after a good look round. Two thrushes came and hopped among the crumbs. Even the wagtail came, wagging his tail up and down in his merry way.

Alice was sitting on the grass, her bag of salt beside her. The birds came nearer and nearer. Alice had a pinch of salt ready. She suddenly threw it among the birds, hoping that some might fall on the tail of one of them. Then it would not be able to fly away and she could pick it up and love it.

But all the birds were scared when Alice raised her hand and threw something. They thought she was throwing a stone, and they flew off with chirrups and squawks. They could not understand why Alice was doing such queer things.

'She always seemed so friendly,' sang the blackbird to the thrush.

'She gives us water to drink and a bowl to splash in,' chirruped the sparrows. 'Why is she throwing things at us today?'

Alice was very upset that all the birds had flown. She went under the lilac bush and had a good cry.

'It's too bad,' she sobbed. 'I do so want to catch a bird by putting salt on its tail, but none of them will let me!'

Now a small elf lived in the bush, and he was most astonished to hear what Alice said. He was fond of the little girl, though she had never seen him – but he had often watched Alice giving food to the birds and pouring fresh water into their bathing bowl.

'Dear me,' he said to himself. 'What a funny thing to cry about! Whoever heard of catching birds by putting salt on their tails? Well, now, I wonder if I can do anything about it?'

Now the elf had a friend. It was the little brown hedge sparrow who had her nest in the hawthorn bush at the end of the garden. When Alice had crept out from the lilac bush to try again with her salt, the elf flew quickly to the hedge sparrow who was sitting on her nest.

'Hedge sparrow,' said the elf, 'will you do something for me?'

'Of course!' said the little brown bird.

'Well, listen,' said the elf. 'There is a little girl in the garden and she wants to catch a bird by putting salt on its tail, and she is very unhappy because she can't. Now do go and hop about in front of her, and let her put salt on your little brown tail. Then let her pick you up and hold you gently against her face so that she can feel how soft and warm you are.'

'But I should be afraid,' said the hedge sparrow in alarm.

'You needn't be,' said the elf. 'She is the kindest girl in this village. Do do it, please.'

'What about my eggs?' asked the hedge sparrow.

'I'll sit on them for a while and keep them warm,' said the elf. So the hedge sparrow flew off and the elf cuddled himself down over the bright blue eggs. Off went the hedge sparrow, still feeling very nervous. She saw Alice sitting patiently on the grass, with her little bag of salt in front of her.

The hedge sparrow flew down and pecked up a crumb. She went nearer and nearer to Alice. Alice took a pinch of salt. Her eyes gleamed with delight. She felt sure she could put some on this little bird's tail!

She threw the salt. It fell on the hedge sparrow's tail like snow. The little bird stayed quite still as if she were caught and could not move. Alice picked her up in her hand.

'Oh!' she cried in delight. 'I've caught a bird at last! Oh, you dear, soft little thing – you are as warm as new-made bread! Oh, how soft you are against my cheek!'

At first the hedge sparrow was afraid, but when she felt how gentle and loving Alice was, she no longer felt nervous. She stayed quite still in the little girl's hand, her tiny heart beating like the quick ticking of a small clock.

'I don't want to hurt or frighten you,' said Alice. 'I only wanted to feel you. Now you shall fly away again. Have you a nest, little bird? How I would love to see it!'

The hedge sparrow flew from Alice's hand and sang her a short sweet burst of song. She flew down the garden and perched on the hawthorn bush to make sure that Alice was following. She wanted to show the little girl her beautiful eggs.

But do you know, when Alice looked for the nest, she saw, first of all, the elf! The hedge sparrow had quite forgotten that the elf had promised to look after her eggs. Alice rubbed her eyes in amazement – and when she took her knuckles from her eyes, the elf was gone. But then Alice saw the four lovely blue eggs shining in the neat brown nest.

'Oh!' she said. 'They are as blue as the sky! Thank you, hedge sparrow, for showing me them. I've never seen such a lovely sight before!'

Alice rushed in to tell her mother – and Uncle Jim was there too.

'Oh, Mother! Oh, Uncle Jim!' cried Alice. 'I caught a bird by putting salt on its tail – and I held it in my hand –and it showed me its nest with four blue eggs in and there was an elf keeping the eggs warm for the bird too!'

How Uncle Jim laughed! 'My dear child,' he said. 'It's just a joke that you can catch birds by putting salt on their tails. You can't really!'

'But I did, I tell you!' cried Alice. 'I did, I did!'

Yes – she certainly did, didn't she? I wonder if you'd be as lucky! You never know!

The Giant's Easter Egg

The Giant's Easter Egg

ONCE UPON a time Buddy the gnome went walking along the highway whistling a merry little tune. As he reached the foot of Wishing Hill, someone came over the top of it.

'My!' said Buddy, in astonishment. 'If that isn't a giant!'

The little gnome walked on and watched the huge giant striding down the hill. As he came nearer, Buddy saw that he carried a great number of baskets.

Whatever's he got in those, I wonder! thought Buddy. *Potatoes perhaps, or boot buttons.*

When the two met, the giant stopped to speak to Buddy.

'Good morning,' he said, in a rumbling voice, putting his baskets down. 'Could you tell me how far I am from Pixie Market in Whispering Wood?'

'Oh, only about half a mile,' answered Buddy, peeping into the giant's baskets. Then he opened his eyes in astonishment.

'Good gracious!' he said. 'What a *tremendous* lot of Easter eggs you've got in your baskets! And what lovely ones they are – chocolate ones and marzipan ones, big ones and little ones, pink ones and white ones! What are you going to do with them all?'

'Sell them at the Pixie Market,' answered the giant. 'Well, I must be off again, or the market will be closed.'

'Oh *do* give me an egg!' begged Buddy, who liked Easter eggs so much that he felt he would like to have eaten them all year round if he could have got them.

'It isn't manners to ask for things like that,' said the giant. 'I *was* going to give you one, but I don't encourage bad manners, so I shan't let you have one. Goodbye.'

And he tramped off, leaving Buddy feeling rather

hot and bothered.

Mean old thing! thought Buddy, as he walked up Wishing Hill. *He might have given me just the teeniest-tiny one, I really do think!*

As he reached the top of the hill, and began going down the other side, he caught sight of something big and brown lying in a hazel tree nearby. He ran up to it to see what it was. Then he danced a little jig in delight.

'It's an Easter egg, an Easter egg, a great big Easter egg!' he chuckled. 'That old giant must have dropped it without knowing it. What a way he'll be in when he finds he's lost his biggest egg! I shan't take it back to Pixie Market till tomorrow, and that will serve him right for not giving me an egg when I asked him!'

The naughty little gnome pulled the egg from the hazel tree, put it on his back, and tramped home with it.

When he got there he put it safely away in his larder. It looked splendid, for it had a broad red ribbon tied round it in a big bow.

I do *wish it was mine!* Buddy kept thinking all the morning. *I'll just go and have a peep at it.*

So he kept peeping at it, and peeping at it, until he began to long to eat it. It smelt so chocolatey and looked so tempting.

Then a naughty thought crept into Buddy's mind. *If I ate just a little bit under the ribbon*, he thought, *no one would ever know.*

So what do you think the bad little gnome did? Why, he took a knife, lifted up the ribbon, and cut a piece right out of the egg!

But just as he was going to pop it into his mouth he dropped the piece of chocolate in an awful fright – for an angry yell came from the egg and it began to roll about on the shelf!

'Oh, oh,' came the voice. 'You've cut me, you've cut me! Let me out, quick!'

Buddy's knees began to shake so that he had to sit down. 'W-w-what is it?' he said. 'Who are you?'

'Oh, let me out!' begged the voice. 'Untie the ribbon, quick! My finger's bleeding!'

Buddy pulled the ribbon undone and then jumped back in fright – for the top part of the egg flew up like a lid, and out jumped a dwarf, looking rather like Humpty-Dumpty, except that he had a long beard. He held one of his fingers in pain, and Buddy saw that the knife must have jabbed it. He quickly bound it up for the queer little dwarf, and asked him to sit down.

'What did you want to wake me up for?' asked the dwarf. 'I belong to the giant, and I make Easter eggs for him once a year, and when I've finished my work I go to sleep again in my own egg until next Easter time. Now you've woken me up I'll have to start making eggs all over again!'

Buddy began to feel excited.

'All right. Go ahead!' he said. 'I'll be only too pleased to have any eggs you can make.'

'You know the rule, don't you?' said the dwarf, rolling up his sleeves. 'No eggs must be left uneaten by tonight, and once I begin making them I shan't stop!'

'Oh, that's all right,' chuckled Buddy. 'You can't make more than *I* can eat!'

The dwarf took an empty bag from his pocket and placed it on the table. He drew a circle round it with a piece of chalk, and then blew on it.

Pop! out rolled a fine fat chocolate egg! Buddy stared as if he couldn't believe his eyes! Then he snatched it up and began eating it. It tasted more delicious than any other egg he had ever eaten. He had only half-eaten it when, pop! out rolled another egg, a marzipan one this time. Buddy thought the little dwarf must be the cleverest magician in the world.

He soon started on the second egg, and found it even more delicious than the first. He was delighted to see the dwarf making more and more eggs of all sizes and colours.

My! he thought. *What a feast I'll have to be sure! And how cross the old giant would be if he knew that I'd found out the secret of his egg-making!*

Buddy began on his third egg. The dwarf by now had made so many that the table was covered with eggs.

'You've made enough for a bit,' said Buddy, 'stop and have a rest.'

'I can't stop, once I've started,' said the dwarf, shaking an enormous egg out of his bag. 'I shall go on until six o'clock this evening.'

'But good gracious! You'll have made about a thousand by then!' cried Buddy in alarm. 'I really couldn't eat a thousand, you know. What would happen if all the eggs weren't eaten by tonight?'

The dwarf chuckled.

'Aha!' he said. 'Then *you'd* have to take my place as egg-maker to the giant, and go back into that big magic egg instead of me!'

Well, that gave Buddy such a shock that all his appetite for eggs seemed to go, and he felt as if he couldn't eat another mouthful. There he sat with big tears in his eyes, watching that horrid dwarf make dozens and dozens of eggs. Soon every chair, table and shelf was full of Easter eggs, and Buddy knew there was only one thing to be done. He must go to the Pixie Market, find the giant, and confess his naughtiness to him.

So off he went, crying large tears all the way. When he got to Pixie Market he saw the giant just packing up his empty baskets to go away. Buddy ran up to him.

'Please!' he said. 'Do come back home with me and get the dwarf who makes your eggs,' and he told the giant all that had happened.

The giant said nothing. He simply put Buddy in a basket, and strode off to the gnome's cottage. And, oh my! The dwarf had made so many Easter eggs that they were rolling out of the cottage door and all along the road!

'Go back to your egg!' the giant thundered to the dwarf. And, hey presto, the dwarf was gone, the great egg clicked to, and there was peace in Buddy's cottage.

'Now,' said the giant to Buddy, 'you can choose which you'd rather do – come and be my servant for a year or having nothing to eat for your meals but Easter eggs until they are all finished.'

'Please, I'll eat the Easter eggs,' said Buddy, thinking he was getting off rather well.

But as there were exactly five hundred and twenty-three eggs to eat, you can guess what Buddy felt like when he sat down a week later to his twenty-second meal of Easter eggs – and found he hadn't eaten even half of them!

'I'll never, *never*, *NEVER* get into mischief again!' he groaned.

And as far as I know he never did!

Acknowledgements

All efforts have been made to seek necessary permissions.

The stories in this publication first appeared in the following publications:

'The Cross Shepherd' first appeared in *Enid Blyton's Sunny Stories*, No. 179, 1940.

'The Disobedient Bunny' first appeared in *The Teacher's Treasury*, Vol. 1, 1926.

'The Easter Chickens' first appeared in *Enid Blyton's Sunny Stories*, No. 66, 1938.

'Mr Quink's Garden' first appeared as 'Mr. Quink's Garden' in *Enid Blyton's Sunny Stories*, No. 72, 1938.

'Slowcoach Sammy' first appeared in *Enid Blyton's Sunny Stories*, No. 191, 1940.

'They Can't Catch Brer Rabbit!' first appeared in *Enid Blyton's Sunny Stories*, No. 377, 1946.

'Biggitty and the Green Hen' first appeared in *Enid Blyton's Sunny Stories*, No. 9, 1937.

'The Runaway Hat' first appeared in *The Teacher's Treasury*, Vol. 1, 1926.

'The Surprising Easter Egg' first appeared in *The Teachers World*, No. 1765, 1937.

'Tick-a-Tock, the Greedy Rabbit' first appeared as 'Tick-A-Tock, the Greedy Rabbit' in *Sunny Stories for Little Folks*, No. 66, 1929.

'Jimmy and the Jackdaw' first appeared in *Enid Blyton's Sunny Stories*, No. 322, 1944.

'First Walk in April – *April Showers*' first appeared in *Enid Blyton's Nature Lover's Book*, 1944.

'The Magic Easter Egg' first appeared in *The Teacher's Treasury*, Vol. 1, 1926.

'The Clock in the Wood' first appeared in *The Teachers World*, No. 1775, 1937.

'The Big Juicy Carrot' first appeared in *Enid Blyton's Sunny Stories*, No. 9, 1937.

'The Queer Little Needles' first appeared in *Enid Blyton's Sunny Stories*, No. 167, 1940.

'The Big Box of Chocolates' first appeared in *Sunny Stories for Little Folks*, No. 209, 1935.

'The Blown-Away Rabbit' first appeared in *Enid Blyton's Sunny Stories*, No. 156, 1940.

'The Top of the Wall' first appeared in *The Teachers World*, No. 1666, 1935.

'Fairy Easter Eggs' first appeared in *The Teachers World*, No. 1087, 1925.

'Goosey-Goosey Gander' first appeared in *Sunny Stories for Little Folks*, No. 147, 1932.

'Snapdragon Snippets' first appeared in *The Teachers World*, No. 1838, 1938.

'Ladybird, Ladybird, Fly Away Home' first appeared in *Sunday Mail*, No. 1918, 1945.

'Jimmy's Robin' first appeared in *Two Years in the Infant School*, Topics 22–42, first published by George Newnes in 1938.

'The Witch's Egg' first appeared in *The Teachers World*, No. 1715, 1936.

'The Wrong Dinnertime' first appeared as 'The Wrong Dinner-Time' in *Enid Blyton's Nature Lover's Book*, 1944.

'Second Walk in April – *Birds in April*' first appeared in *Enid Blyton's Nature Lover's Book*, 1944.

'The Buttercup Spell' first appeared in *Enid Blyton's Magazine*, No. 11, 1956.

'Salt on a Bird's Tail' first appeared in *Enid Blyton's Sunny Stories*, No. 152, 1939.

'The Giant's Easter Egg' first appeared in *The Teachers World*, No. 1150, 1926.

Join the Adventure

THE FAMOUS FIVE

Five on a Treasure Island

Five Run Away Together

Five Go to Smuggler's Top

Five Go Off in a Caravan

Five on Kirrin Island Again

Five Go Off to Camp

Five Get into Trouble

Five Fall into Adventure

Five on a Hike Together

Five Have a Wonderful Time

Five Go Down to the Sea

Five Go to Mystery Moor

Five Have Plenty of Fun

Five on a Secret Trail

Five Go to Billycock Hill

Five Get Into a Fix

Five on Finniston Farm

Five Go to Demon's Rocks

Five Have a Mystery to Solve

Five Are Together Again

Have you read them all?

Enid Blyton

is one of the most popular children's authors of all time. Her books have sold over 500 million copies and have been translated into other languages more often than any other children's author.

Enid Blyton adored writing for children. She wrote over 600 books and hundreds of short stories. *The Famous Five* books, now 75 years old, are her most popular. She is also the author of other favourites including *The Secret Seven*, *The Magic Faraway Tree*, *Malory Towers* and *Noddy*.

Born in London in 1897, Enid lived much of her life in Buckinghamshire and adored dogs, gardening and the countryside. She was very knowledgeable about trees, flowers, birds and animals.

Dorset – where some of the Famous Five's adventures are set – was a favourite place of hers too.

Enid Blyton's stories are read and loved by millions of children (and grown-ups) all over the world. Visit enidblyton.co.uk to discover more.